Mississippi River Dreams

Coming of Age in the 1850's

by

Mary Charlotte Aubry Costello

With illustrations by the Author

This book is dedicated
to the children in my life:
my six -
Pat, Barb, Judy, Tom, Roger and John
and my former students at McKinley School,
Davenport, Iowa.

MISSISSIPPI RIVER DREAMS
Coming of Age in the 1850's

Publisher - Mary C. Costello
Designer - Bob Grove
Printer - J & A Printing, Inc.
Illustrator - Mary C. Costello

Library of Congress Catalog Card Number *(Applied For)*
ISBN 0-9644518-4-0 Softcover

First Edition: June 2004

Manufactured in the United States of America

Cover: *This scene, from 22 April 1856, depicts a train crossing the
newly finished railroad bridge for the first time. The novel characters are
among the crowd greeting it. Erin, waving, is next to Colleen and James,
their father; but Maura, their mother, was separated from them and is
looking for her family.*

Table of Contents

Acknowledgments

I wish to thank those people who have helped make this book possible, in the order in which things occurred.

Thanks to my son **Roger** for his encouragement at the very beginning when I told him of the many interesting historical events that had happened in this area. His thinking that it could be a bestseller instilled confidence in me to begin, and his "checking" weekly has kept me on schedule.

Thanks to my daughter **Judith**, who has helped with copy suggestions the whole year and even experimented with the bead-making to prove it works. Her time-consuming and meticulous proofing helped to bind the copy into what I hope is a tight, well-knit book.

Pat, my oldest son, has always been there (day and night) to answer computer problems without getting upset with my ignorance of this electronic miracle. Later, despite time restrictions, he proofed the copy and found some major corrections.

Teri (Alice Ann) Ryan, now deceased, provided the Irish family name (Kane) while she was confined to her hospital bed.

Sarah Wesson, special collections librarian at the Davenport Library, jokingly claims to be part-author of this book since she did most of the research into the 1850's lifestyle. Then later she proofed the manuscript and provided excellent suggestions and corrections.

Becca Costello, my granddaughter-in-law and a busy mother, spent most of one Sunday helping me with my computer.

Sister Kathleen Eberdt, CHM, assisted with proofing of the copy and critiquing of the artwork, but mostly was very encouraging and supportive through the whole process.

My thanks to *Rochelle Murray*, Davenport Library Children's Librarian, for evaluating the book for the age a child might read it, and for her review.

Lastly, I can't thank *Suzanne Hartung* enough for all her time, energy and proofreading/editing expertise given voluntarily to make the book a success. Without her I never would have made the deadline. I am truly grateful.

A Special Thanks
to
Mary Priester
For believing in this project
And being the "Angel"
To make this happen.

Author's Note

Although the historical facts presented herein are accurate, I have taken the license to change the details surrounding them, and sometimes the dates have been changed to fit the evolving story.

For example, John Deere and a friend discovered an arsonist about to burn the bridge in August of 1860, instead of 1856, as I have suggested. And Captain Harris purchased his new boat, the *Grey Eagle*, too late in 1857 to have opened the riverboat season that year as I portray him. There really ***was*** a teacher in Public School #2, in Rock Island, who taught from 1836 until 1854. There ***were*** eleven runaways from one family in the south in the time period that I suggest. Ben Brayton ***did*** confirm the story that he saw and talked with Abraham Lincoln on 1 September 1857, although some stories question that Lincoln came to the area at that time.

Setting the Scene

The date is 1854. Franklin Pierce is President. There is great unrest between the North and South over slavery.

A 45-year-old man by the name of Abraham Lincoln is gaining prestige with his law practice in Springfield, Illinois. The Sauk and Fox Indians have been forced off their home at Saukenauk Village on the Rock River and their hunting grounds surrounding it along the Mississippi. Most were annihilated in the Black Hawk War of 1832. The remaining members of the tribe were sent to Tama, Iowa.

The railroad is moving westward from Chicago to Rock Island, Illinois. A bridge is being constructed on the Mississippi River at Rock Island to connect the East to the West.

The Kane family has settled in Rock Island, after having moved 4,000 miles from County Tipperary, Ireland, four years prior.

Here is where our story begins.

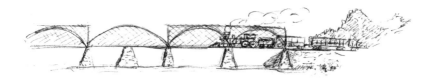

Chapter 1
LOST
Wednesday, 22 February 1854

"I'm so excited! The Iron Horse comes today!" exclaimed Colleen Kane. Her heart raced, for she knew something special would be happening today for the residents of Rock Island, Illinois, and surrounding areas in Iowa.

"Can I go see the horse?" asked her brother, Erin.

"It's not a horse," Colleen said impatiently. "People call it the Iron Horse because it has taken the place of horses. It's bigger than a horse and is made of iron. It is really a train run by an engine that blows out steam and smoke... kind of like a horse snorting. It runs on tracks that Papa has helped lay from Chicago to the new railroad station here in Rock Island." She paused. "I can't wait to see it."

Erin was confused but didn't say more. He liked horses but didn't know if he'd like an iron one.

"Do you know what day it is?" asked Colleen.

"Yes, it's the day the Iron Horse is coming," responded Erin, thinking it a trick question.

"No, silly, I mean the date. What date is it?"

"How would I know?" Erin was getting upset with his sister's questions.

"It is the 22nd of February! Do you know whose birthday it is?" Colleen questioned her brother, who was really not too interested by now.

"No, but I'm sure you will tell me."

"It is George Washington's birthday. My teacher says that there are some people living today who remember him alive. Papa says that is why the railroad wants the first train to arrive today. People will always remember this day." Colleen was twelve but felt much older and wiser than her brother. After all, he was only eight. "It's really cold outside, but Papa said we can go see the train," commented Colleen.

The children's mother, Maura, was fixing a noon meal and told them to wash up. They used the large bowl on the side of the fireplace filled with water heated over the fireplace coals. The warm water felt good because the house was drafty with the north wind blowing outside.

1

They had homemade bread, grape jelly and milk. As a treat, their mother gave them each a cookie.

"Mamma, when does the train get to Rock Island?" asked Colleen as she picked up the last cookie crumb from the wooden table.

"Faith and begorrah, child, it has a long way to come, and it will be picking up many important people, like Governor Matteson, mayor of the Big City, railroad officials and many more. Your father said it would arrive at six o'clock. He says trains are always on time. We are to meet him there."

Maura was very excited but wasn't showing it. She knew that this event might mean job security for her husband on the railroad for a long time. Things were happening fast. Some track had already been laid on ground on the other side of the mighty Mississippi River in Davenport, Iowa, headed toward Iowa City, in anticipation of a bridge being built between the two states.

"What can we do now?" whined Erin.

Maura thought for a moment, then went to the cupboard for a loaf of sugar and two small bowls. She crumbled about a half cup of sugar into each container, being careful not to spill any, and added a tablespoon full of flour to each. She had the children stir the two together till the flour vanished. Then she poured into each mixture a little beet juice she had saved from last night's meal.

"Stir the juice into the sugar," she said, "and see what happens."

"How pretty!" exclaimed Colleen when she saw the rich pink result.

"Oh, mine is red, Mamma! Thank you," shouted Erin, delighted at the sight.

"Now take a little of the mix in your hand and roll it into a ball," instructed their mother. "You are going to make beads for a bracelet or necklace. Before they are dry, you can make a hole with a darning needle so they can be strung on a string."

The children got so involved in making beads of different sizes that the time passed swiftly. At 5 o'clock, Maura announced that the children should leave the beads to dry on the newspaper and get washed up to go meet Papa and see the train.

They dressed warmly because, though the sun had been out, the temperature was freezing. Colleen donned a well-worn sweater over her wool jumper and a cape her mother had cut down from her own. Erin covered up with his birthday sweater that his mother had knitted from leftover yarn. Maura put on her patched red plaid cape of wool, done so beautifully that the casual observer would not know it had

2

Erin and Colleen making beads

3

been repaired. Little did Maura know that a new cape was the first thing that her husband planned to give her when there was money to spare.

As the three stepped outside their small house they could hear the gentle lapping of the river, which was just a stone's throw away but was starting to freeze. "If Illinois Street didn't turn, it would be at our back door, and then go into the Mississippi," Maura used to say laughingly when telling friends where they lived.

The new railroad depot was six blocks away. People were coming from three directions, all headed for the depot -- some walking, others on horseback or in a buggy. The Kanes were surprised at the number of people and hoped that they would find a place not too far away from the ceremony so they could see. Maura suggested that they hold hands so they wouldn't be separated or be hit by a wagon or a horse frightened by the activity.

James had promised to meet them at the freight house, which was a little closer to the river. The crowds there were smaller and the people less elegantly dressed. The children saw their father and ran up to him. James was still in his work clothes because, as he explained, his crew had just finished laying the track to the depot an hour earlier. Although they had planned to be done before today, no one could foresee the many days of heavy snowfall in January. James was foreman of the track-laying crew and pushed the men as hard as he could. But only so much could be done each day in the bitter cold. People had started to gather while the crew was still driving the last spikes.

James greeted his family by swinging Erin around in a circle and giving Colleen a big hug. Maura got a loving kiss.

"I was beginning to worry that you wouldn't make it on time," exclaimed James. "'Number 10' will be on time to the minute! In fact, I think I can hear its whistle now." With the band playing and the excited citizens yelling to each other, it was hard to hear anything else. Then the band stopped and people could hear the whistle and see the Iron Horse coming down the track with its smoke billowing up into the sky, a bunting and garlands of greenery blowing around the centered oil-headlight coming like a charging one-eyed monster.

Both sides of the track were lined with people and the train passengers were hanging out the windows waving flags, the women using their handkerchiefs to show their exuberance. People were shouting, the band started playing "Hail Columbia," and the engineer blew the train whistle.

Everyone knew that this was a great moment. It was the beginning of a new era for the country.

But it was too much for Erin. He let go of his parents' hands and covered his ears. His parents smiled at each other to see his reaction.

The crowd was pushing from behind to get closer to the decorated engine as it halted its magnificent arrival with a great plume of smoke from the giant black funnel above and released steam from its huge coupled wheels on the track.

The family got separated. Erin wanted to see the "horse" up close. Weaving in and out of people, he found himself right next to the big black "iron horse," as Colleen had called it. "It doesn't look like a horse at all," he thought. "I wonder what it's like inside."

The engineer was leaning out of his cab window and the fireman was behind him in the short coal car. Next was a man in a dark uniform with gold buttons and matching beaked cap, holding a lantern, standing next to the bottom step of the coach, helping people out of the first car to the ground. Erin kept walking toward the back of the train. People were deboarding – women in their long rustling skirts and fancy big hats and men dressed up like he had never seen before, in top hats and shiny vests. A man in a dark suit with two square red flags tucked under his arm was helping ladies from another of the railroad cars.

Erin walked farther and found that the fourth car was empty of its passengers and the crowd was heading for the depot. Ever so adroitly Erin climbed the first giant step and the few remaining ones into the passenger car.

Once his eyes adjusted to the dim lighting, he could see that it was messy and dirty because the windows were open and the soot from the coal-burning engine ahead had blown in. There were newspapers and crumpled, greased paper which originally had held lunches but now contained apple cores and crumbs. Those people who had been traveling all day had brought food along and had left the garbage when they got off. Rummaging through the debris, Erin even found a cookie. . . and ate it!

He was surprised to see the layout. An aisle went down the center of the car with highback seats big enough for two people on either side. Some were facing each other, making a perfect space, he thought, to play hide-and-seek. There were oil lamps lit overhead, for it was getting dark outside.

Erin was so absorbed in his discoveries that he had forgotten about his parents and his sister. But now, with darkness setting in, he was starting to feel uneasy.

Suddenly he heard someone coming. It was a black man in a white uniform, singing to himself as he carried a large white canvas bag into which he was placing trash. Erin crouched down and hid between the seats. Now he wished he had never gotten on the train.

Outside by the railroad depot, Colleen and her parents were frantic. They had missed Erin when the crowd thinned out. Most of the revelers had gone into the depot for the reception that was to be held there. The Kanes called Erin's name and asked friends if they had seen him. No one remembered seeing the boy. James went up to the trainmen and asked if they had seen a red-haired boy, eight years old, around the train. No one had. Then the brakeman recalled seeing a lad going down the boardwalk toward the end of the train.

Immediately Colleen felt that Erin was on board the train. She knew how curious her brother was, and thought he would want to explore. She told her father, who told the conductor, and a search began. They started with the first car behind the coal car. It was quite dark inside even with the overhead lamps, so the conductor brought his lantern and shone it into all corners of the passenger car. Everyone called Erin's name, but with no results. They searched the next two cars without finding him. Then they reached the fourth car, where the porter, stooped over, was still cleaning up the seats and floor and closing the open windows which had made it very cold in the train. Erin was near the back, hiding, but when he heard his sister calling, he sheepishly came out.

Colleen saw him first and screamed, "There he is!" Everybody looked ahead and frowns gave way to smiles. Everyone wanted to hug him at once, but with the narrow aisle, that was impossible. Colleen took his hand and headed for the exit sign and down the steps, jumping the last big one and hitting the ground hard. Thanking the conductor, who also had been worried, James helped Maura down from the car and the family headed for home, with Erin being scolded the whole way for putting the family through such worry.

Chapter 2
CELEBRATION
Wednesday evening, 22 February 1854

As the happy group walked down the track toward their humble home, they passed two more empty cars, a second engine and five more passenger cars. The crowds were much larger than even James had expected. The Kanes heard the steam engine whistle blow behind them – a loud "woo-woo" once, then many times, as the evening progressed.

James told the children and Maura about the railroad executives he recognized – Sheffield, Buford and Henry Farnam, President and Chief Engineer of the railroad, who had congratulated and thanked him that evening for accomplishing what two days ago had seemed impossible. The track-laying from Moline (James's responsibility for the last two months) was a key to the success of this day and Farnam knew it. James had been invited to the big reception, but he felt he didn't have the proper clothes to wear, so he had declined the invitation.

Later James learned that whenever a speaker at the great celebration gave a toast, a man posted by the door gave the engineer a signal to blow the train whistle. It was all very exciting for the reveler, but for a family trying to unwind and get to bed and sleep, it was a nuisance.

Before he tucked his son into bed, James had a serious talk with Erin about wandering away from his family as he had done this evening.

"We thank the Good Lord for your safety, Erin! Your mother and sister and I were very concerned that you might have been trampled in the crowd or lured away by a stranger. Many things crossed our minds in the time you were missing, lad. We love you very much and need to know where you are at all times. You cannot wander off like that!" James was firm and serious.

"But, Papa! The noise was so loud and the people were pushing so hard I needed to get away. I am sorry if I worried you. I won't do it again." Erin was remorseful at the moment as his father tucked the sheet and blanket up under his chin. But he had enjoyed his little adventure on the new puffing monster of a train and was glad he got to see it inside. He thought someday he might be the one to drive an Iron Horse. As an afterthought he said, "Papa, what do you call the man who runs the train?"

"An engineer, Erin, but you get some sleep now. Say your prayers, son, and tomorrow will be here before you know it. May God let you sleep well."

In their small, one-room house, Maura, who had already said good night to Erin, was at the table examining the beads the children had made, which were drying on the red-stained newspaper and sparkling in the candlelight.

Colleen had gotten ready for bed behind a screen that James had constructed from scrap wood left behind by carpenters when they were building the depot. The construction workers had even given him a few long pieces of pine. The twelve-year-old, conscious of her blooming womanhood, had been so embarrassed when getting dressed and undressed before her parents and brother, that with Maura's encouragement, her father had put together a simple hinged frame which Maura then covered with a patchwork of clothing scraps from her "piece bag." Many of these materials brought back memories to Maura of her earlier times as a young girl – the dress she wore at her first Communion in Ireland, her coat on the long cold journey by boat to America, her mother's favorite green corduroy dress and many more. The screen was Colleen's Christmas present last year and one that she dearly loved. The same type of patchwork covered the three beds as quilts, though in smaller, even shapes. This gave color to what otherwise would have been a drab dwelling.

The rough-hewn table in the middle of the space with two solid high-backed chairs and two padded-top barrels for stools, and a tall cherry wood chest of drawers by the parents' double bed (Maura's one purchased piece of furniture and her pride and joy) completed the original furniture in the Kane home. An open hearth at the bottom of the chimney was where Maura cooked, and an iron teakettle and her few pots and pans were prominent there.

On a free wall opposite their double bed was a single painting of their homeland that Maura treasured. The artist's name she did not know, but the scene reminded her of early happy days in Ireland, with the lush, green grass interspersed with rock and the beautiful River Shannon.

She had been given the painting by friends who were moving and couldn't take everything. Along with the painting, she had acquired a candle box large enough to hold candles for a year. (It was never full but kept the few that Maura had on hand from becoming deformed in the heat of the hearth or a hot summer day.) The last and most useable piece was a pedestal rocker with a horsehide upholstered seat in which guests could sit or James could relax at the end of the day. It was strong, serviceable and comfortable and something she never would have been able to afford to buy, so she was most grateful.

As the Kane family settled down to sleep, they could hear the celebrations in the town continuing into the night with bonfires, illuminated public buildings and even some private celebrations, both in Rock Island and across the river in Davenport. There was even a grand ball at the LeClaire House in downtown Davenport. "Never had the area been so lit up and beautiful," said Henry Farnam to James later.

Chapter 3
NEW FRIENDS
Sunday, 26 February 1854

It was Sunday and, as was the routine in the Kane family, when the priest – who served a large area surrounding Rock Island – was in town, they were all up early to get ready to go to Mass at 9:30. Saint James Church was on the corner of Rock River and Dock Streets, only about 7 blocks from their house. They were so happy to have a Catholic Church nearby.

James remembered well the first year they arrived in Rock Island. Because there was no Catholic Church on the Illinois side of the river, they and the other Catholic families in the area made the big trek by boat to Davenport, Iowa – crossing the slough first, then the river. When the river was frozen, why, they walked on the ice!

Jutting between those bodies of water was the end of the island. There they would often meet folks who lived on the island or even people coming from Moline who had crossed a dam to the island. All were headed to St. Anthony's Church in Davenport, which had been built by Antoine LeClaire in 1838.

Getting to church became much easier when St. James Church in Rock Island was built by Father John G. Alleman in 1851. The good Father was a big man in splendid health who, it is said, could cover as much ground in a morning on foot as an average horse. When new Catholics moved into the area, he always paid them a visit and, blessed with a terrific memory, he never forgot their names.

Father Alleman had visited the Kanes after he first arrived. Colleen told her friends, "My parents were disappointed that he was French, not Irish, but they came to know him to be a friendly, devout person and they became great friends. Papa helped on weekends and on long summer evenings to build St. James Church, the first Catholic Church in Rock Island County." The parish grew very fast, with people moving into the area every day.

Today, as the Kanes walked along Dock Street, they met other families doing the same. Still others came by horse and wagon or buggy from Moline or even greater distances. Father Alleman greeted all at the door of the church. "Good morning, James and Maura! And how are you, Colleen and Erin?" Colleen felt so very grown-up. "It was a big event last Wednesday with the train arriving," Father continued. "I

13

hear you finished spiking the track just in time, James!" Father Alleman had picked up the appropriate terminology from talking to Papa. "We are all grateful to you. This will bring more souls to our town and our church."

Father Alleman then greeted the Ryans, who were behind the Kane family. James found a pew near the front of the church and all genuflected before filing into their seats. Maura had taught the children that bowing on bended knee shows honor to God, who is always in the Catholic Church, as is shown by a sanctuary candle that is never allowed to go out. Maura entered the pew first, then Erin, Colleen and, lastly, Papa.

They were there but a few minutes when the Gannons filled the pew behind. Mr. Gannon whispered something to Papa before Mass started, but Colleen was more aware that among the five Gannon children was a boy a little older than she. She glanced quickly at him as he followed his younger brothers to fill up the seat, and then she noticed that he was looking at her. Embarrassed, Colleen turned back to the altar. Her face was flushed so she didn't look behind again.

Father Alleman gave a long sermon on the Prodigal Son and related it to God's love and forgiveness for all. At Communion time the Kane family went up to the altar railing to receive Communion, and Colleen caught the Gannon boy's eye again. "Why does he make me feel warm and funny? I have never felt like this before," she thought.

After Mass was over, everyone filed out of church, and James stopped to talk to Mr. Gannon, who also worked for the railroad. James wanted to know when the bridge might be completed across the river. Mr. Gannon replied that it would be next year, barring delays. That was bad news, because James knew that meant he would be out of work until then, but Mr. Gannon had other information that he wished to discuss with James. The two men agreed to meet in the morning at the freight house.

Before the Gannons left in their horse and wagon, the younger Gannon boys piled into the back of the wagon. But the oldest son – whose name, Colleen had overheard, was Tom – helped his mother up onto the seat next to his father. This spontaneous act of courtesy was not missed by Colleen.

Chapter 4
WORK
Monday, 27 February 1854

It was cold in the house. James woke up early and stoked the fire in the fireplace. He was very eager to meet with Bill Gannon about finding work.

He tried to be quiet as he moved about the room. On the table was a loaf of Maura's delicious homemade bread, wrapped in a towel, and beside it a jar of grape jam. He filled the tall coffee pot with water collected from the cistern, added coffee beans which Maura had ground up, and set the pot on top of the grate in the fireplace to heat. By this time, Maura had risen from sleep and put on her robe. She fixed him two eggs and potatoes in her iron fry-pan.

When he finished eating, James dressed for subzero weather and walked toward the meeting place, the freight house. The sun was just rising behind him, giving him hope that the news from Gannon would be good. God had always taken care of him in his needs...and he and his family certainly needed Him to find a job!

James had a strong work ethic developed in his youth. In Ireland, when he was only eight, Erin's age, both James's father and his older brother had died, and James had gone to work to support his mother and younger siblings. He had many scars to show for it, but he always had found work to do. "Yes, the sun is up and God is looking down on me. This will be my lucky day," he thought to himself as he took giant steps along the rugged ground next to the railroad track.

Bill Gannon had arrived just minutes before. "Top of the mornin' to you, James," he said, "and it is a good one." The two men didn't waste time but got right down to business.

Bill Gannon explained, "The railroad bridge is started. The piers were set in the Sylvan Slough last fall, and now John Warren is working on the superstructure."

"In the meantime," he continued, "the M&M Railroad, formed by a group of locals, has started to lay track on the Iowa side of the river. We'll be ready for westward travel when the bridge is complete. Every day people are flocking into Davenport and the area by boat or train, looking to go West. Gold in California has people getting feverish! Our foreman has quit. So, James, could you head the crew of men to do this work?"

James couldn't believe his ears. "Of course I can do that! When do you want me to start?"

Mr. Gannon wanted to show James where the materials were and what had been done on the track so far. The two men took Gannon's horse and wagon to the ferry, which was only a few blocks away. This being late February, the season had not yet opened for the ferry but the ice on the river was still very thick, so the men decided to drive the wagon across.

Arriving at the Davenport ferry landing, they drove to the beginning of the M&M Railroad track. They were surprised to be met by Antoine LeClaire and Henry Farnam. The stockpile of railroad track supplies that had come by boat last fall from St. Louis was nearby. After introductions were made, Mr. LeClaire congratulated James on his completion of the tracks for the historic first train. He had heard from Farnam of James's last-minute push to beat the train.

Then Gannon told them that James had agreed to head the crew of track-layers for the M&M Railroad. Both men were very pleased and they discussed the timeline.

James learned from Gannon that the crew had not gone very far with the track because of the difficulty in getting the materials to the place where they were needed. The heavy creosote-treated ties, barrels of spikes and iron rails were stockpiled on the levee in Davenport. Carrying this material by horse and wagon was not efficient. James said that a railroad engine was needed to move the materials to the work location. He suggested that with the river still frozen solid, they could bring an engine from the island across on the ice. Mr. Gannon liked James's proposal.

That night Maura was delighted to hear of James's work offer. She also was impressed that he had met Antoine LeClaire. Everyone knew of Mr. LeClaire and she remembered the boat trips across the river to "his" church, St. Anthony's in Davenport. LeClaire had contributed the land and money to build the first Catholic Church in the area sixteen years ago, as he had done for other denominations since. St. Anthony's was now building a larger church, on the same site, to accommodate the influx of immigrants. Maura had seen LeClaire at Mass with his wife, Marguerite, but had never met him, nor did she ever expect to.

For the railroad to accomplish what James had suggested – that is, bringing a train across the frozen Mississippi – an engine, tender and flatcar were made available on the island. A farmer with oxen was located. The whole operation was questioned by many. James, however, maintained confidence that this could be done.

When he informed his family that evening, Erin begged, "Can I go see the train slide across the river on ice, Papa? Please? Please?"

"Erin, it will probably be a school day, and I don't know what time the oxen and the engine will be ready. And Glory be but it will be bitter cold out there, as well. You shouldn't be out in that cold when it is not necessary."

"Oh, Papa, it sounds like something I might never see again. You said the oxes will pull the big engine on the ice. Won't the heavy engine break the ice?"

"First, Erin, it is 'oxen,' and secondly, no, the recent cold wave has produced unusually thick ice. For that 25-ton engine I figure 24 to 30 inches would be plenty thick. But we can't wait long or a thaw could make it impossible. Ramps need to be built down to the river. That is our problem now. I have crews on both sides of the river working on that. Then we need a big, sturdy pallet with runners for the engine to be pulled on."

Maura was listening to this exchange as she cleaned up after the evening meal. For the first time she spoke up.

"Erin, I'm sorry, but as your father said, if it's a school day, 'No!' Your father can tell you all about it after it is over."

The very disappointed Erin went to his bed after that and buried his head in its quilt-cover, not wanting anyone to see the tears. He knew there was no use in arguing.

James Kane was in charge of the operation to get the engine safely across the river. He checked the depth of the ice himself to make sure the thickness was great enough. He used an auger to cut a hole down to the water in the main channel. By poking a stick in the hole and measuring it against his boot length, he determined the ice was close to two feet. Near the riverbanks it was all the way up to 30 inches thick.

The ramp and track were ready Tuesday on the Illinois island side of the river, but on the Iowa side there were more problems. The already-laid M&M track was further from the river, and the businesses that were building along the riverfront needed to be avoided. Other men created the long, sturdy pallet out of split logs, flat-side up, fastened together, with track on top and runners on the bottom. Despite problems, the greatest being the bitter cold, James was able to get everything ready for the "big move" by Friday.

Antoine LeClaire, William Gannon and other M&M Railroad officials were on hand on the Iowa shore to observe this spectacular event. The big, black engine with its tall smokestack was fired up on the island shore and ran down the ramp with tender and flat-car attached. At the ramp end, the pallet track accepted the "John Dix" locomotive on board. The engineer stopped the engine, and the locomotive and tender were uncoupled from the flatbed car. A special connection James devised secured the heavy vehicle, and the oxen were chained to the pallet runners. The engineer and fireman let the team of oxen take over. With the farmer to direct and encourage the animals, slowly the great iron monster slid across the ice, accompanied by the shouts of the bystanders.

When they reached the main channel, near the center of the river, the enormous cargo began to slide to one side, pulling the sure-footed oxen off balance. Onlookers and workers alike held their breath until the oxen slowly gained control again.

There were no more problems the rest of the way until the crucial lining up of the pallet with the track in Davenport. It had to be precise. The farmer stopped and started and moved the muscular animals until the pallet track was lined up exactly with the track on land. A little extra heave of the oxen, reconnecting by the special crew, and the engine was fired up again and driven up the ramp.

The number of observers had picked up until by now there was a crowd, who yelled and waved as the engine climbed the gradual incline and waited for the railroad car to be transported across. Then the engine was coupled with the car and climbed to ground level ready for work in Iowa. What a magnificent accomplishment that was!

James remembered every detail to tell Erin, Colleen and Maura that night around the dinner table.

"Oh, how thrilling just to imagine, but to see it must have been almost beyond belief!" commented Colleen.

"Glory be to God, but I am so proud of you, James! I wonder if anything like this has ever been done before?" Maura, getting up to serve bread pudding for dessert, went behind James and gave him a big hug.

"Out East probably someone has had to resort to such an answer, though I haven't heard of it," humbly responded James, who was very pleased with his family's reactions. Personally he was exhausted but extremely happy to have the event safely over.

Erin exclaimed, "I told Mr. McGregor, our teacher, about it today, but he said even if the classes went down to the Rock Island shoreline, we wouldn't be able to see much because of the distance. It would be better to be in Davenport or on the island for a view. Besides my friends didn't want to go and stand in the cold." Erin finally had consoled himself that just hearing about it, rather than being out in the freezing cold, was best.

Monday, the piles of rails and ties were loaded onto the flatcar and were taken to the end of the already-laid track. Besides having them available for the workers, there was another reason for moving the supplies. Rock Island and Davenport were riverboat towns, and the boat people were fully aware that the railroad was going to cut into their business. Some would do anything to stop the bridge and the railroad. So Antoine LeClaire had enlisted guards for the construction supplies until James was able to remove those endangered materials from the riverfront.

Chapter 5
MIRACLE
Friday, 3 March 1854

No one lived as close to the river as Colleen and Erin Kane. Everything was across the tracks! The weather was extremely cold in the winter, especially bad on windy days, but every other season they loved their location. The sunrises and sunsets were unobstructed views no artist could paint. Moonlight reflecting on the flowing river caused the poet in Colleen to spring eloquent: "Shimmering, gleaming, beaming, glistening, glimmering, sometimes glassy." She loved to write, and subjects along the river inspired her.

Colleen and Erin walked to their schoolhouse in every kind of weather. After crossing the tracks, they met their friends and still had a good mile down Orleans Street. School was a block beyond Courthouse Square.

Colleen's school assignment for today was to write, "What I Hope My Future Will Bring." She had been thinking about this subject for a long time and was pleased with the composition she had written.

John McGregor was the teacher at Rock Island Public School Number 2, where Colleen and Erin attended, beginning in 1836 when the town was called Stephenson, and he had remained dedicated to his profession for 18 years. In winter, before the students arrived, he was expected to clear the school entrance of snow, if necessary, chop the wood or bring it in from a stockpile, and start a fire in the pot-bellied stove to heat the one-room school.

Colleen described Mr. McGregor as an 'Uncle Sam type' – tall, thin, prim, very erect and proper, with greying hair, always dressed up with vest and coat and crossed tie. His mouth was usually drawn straight and tight, but his brown eyes sparkled to see his students get his point or succeed in any fashion.

Although the schoolmaster was kind and understanding, he could be severe if the occasion demanded – for example, the time Josiah and Ben fought during recess. Benjamin, a boy big for his age, loved to pick on Josiah, who was small and frail. This day, Josiah's Jewish faith was the occasion. "Jew boy, Jew boy, you don't even know what Sunday is!" Ben taunted him almost nose to nose, until Josiah swung his clenched fist at his opponent, hitting him in the face. It was so unexpected that Ben reeled a little and then went after Josiah, getting him on the ground and pummeling him good. Mr. McGregor heard the commotion and was out in a heartbeat to separate the boys, both of whom ended up with colorful bruises and stern reprimands. A talk on religious tolerance was the class's history lesson for the day.

Today was Friday, an exciting day because Mr. McGregor always ended the week of reading, writing and arithmetic with a spelling bee. Both the Kane children were good spellers and enjoyed the challenge.

But the day had just begun. Mr. McGregor rung the hand-held bell as he held open the door, admitting the 21 students to the single-room building. After everyone had hung their coats on hooks in the entry hall and deposited their metal lunch pails on the shelf above so as not to attract mice, some students sat in double desks. For Benjamin and two other big boys, the seats were too small, so they had single desks but their legs extended into the aisles and even farther if they slouched.

Roll call indicated that all were present, and the schoolmaster announced an essay contest sponsored by the Rock Island Railroad on the need for the railroad bridge. Mr. McGregor encouraged all students fourth grade and up to enter. It was a city-wide contest, with both Rock Island schools participating and the winner to receive a free trip to Chicago by train. Last week, the Riverboat Association had announced a similar contest on the importance of steamboats to the economy. Mr. McGregor felt that he could not be accused of taking sides, having both issues represented. Actually, he had spoken to Henry Farnam and had set up the railroad contest with fairness in mind.

The daily routine progressed as usual, with reading first, in groups of different levels. Colleen was in the top level with a long-legged boy named Donald Swenson. Colleen and Donald helped with the younger students and practiced their skills by reading portions of a book aloud to the whole school while the schoolmaster graded papers. Colleen loved to do that because she could be dramatic at times or change her voice for effect.

Arithmetic was next and each student brought out an abacus – a wooden frame with rows of beads sliding back and forth on rods or wires. All students learned their addition, subtraction, multiplication and division on this instrument. Here is where the boys showed their skills. Erin learned to use the abacus with precision right from the beginning, and although he was only in third grade, he could add and subtract almost any number with it. He was anxious for the greater challenge of multiplication.

After recess, Colleen expected that Mr. McGregor would collect their compositions and her heart beat quickly! She was quite pleased with

Erin and the rescued "Miracle"

what she had written and hoped that the master would be as well. The boys behind her had been pulling on her pigtails, which distracted her when Mr. McGregor asked her to pick up the homework.

"Colleen, did you hear me? Would you pick up the compositions?" Mr. McGregor asked again.

"Yes, sir!" she responded as she gladly stood up to get away from her tormentors.

She picked up the notebooks in which the children kept their assignments. Some were neat and clean, while others were well-decorated with the children's artwork, and one was very wet on the outside from lying in the snow while its owner had a snowball fight.

The schoolmaster had written on the blackboard a handwriting assignment, and while the students were practicing their 'shadow writing,' he graded the homework.

"When I grow up, I want to be a farmer like my pa," was a common response with most of the students, adding reasons such as "because I love the outdoors," or "I enjoy the smell of the new-mown hay," or "I like seeing the pigs wallowing in the mud." Some were written in poor English or with incorrect spelling. Abigail wanted to be a seamstress like her mother. The blacksmith's son wanted to follow in his father's footsteps and create things in iron. One very poor girl said she wanted to marry a rich man and travel around the world with him. Erin, at the moment, wanted to be a schoolmaster like Mr. McGregor.

"Colleen, come up here, please," said the schoolmaster.

"It appears that you have spent quite a bit of time on this paper, Colleen. Did you have help from your parents?" he quizzed her.

"No, sir, my parents expect me to do my best in everything, but they don't do things for me," was Colleen's shocked response.

Just then there was a loud crash, broken glass, loud clucking, feathers flying, blood spattering, children screaming and total chaos. The schoolmaster sat in shock for a moment – he couldn't speak or move from his high seat. But he quickly assessed what had happened.

"Children!" he demanded in his loudest, most authoritative voice to quiet them down. "Come over here away from the window. Be careful of the glass! Is anyone hurt?"

Theresa, the seamstress's daughter, started crying because flying glass had cut her arm. Joseph, one of the big eighth graders, had a cut on his forehead that was bleeding profusely, and Erin had picked up a shard of glass from his desk and cut his finger.

Mr. McGregor ordered Colleen to get clean rags from a bag he kept for any emergency, while he, himself, got the water pail and dipper always kept in the room for drinking water. He dabbed clean water over the cuts to get out any glass and with clean cloths tried to stop the bleeding. Then he bound up the wounds with clean cloth pads held in place with strips of material that Colleen had torn.

In the meantime, he ordered Jim to sweep the glass into a pile and big Benjamin to get that piece of tin from behind the bookcase and cover the window as best he could. "Don't get cut on the glass," he cautioned. Some semblance of order was returning except for the cause of the catastrophe. The bloody, apparently dead, chicken lay with a rock attached on the schoolhouse floor. The children all took turns examining the carcass and asking why would someone do this. Mr. McGregor's mind was racing to try to find this answer himself.

Was there a disgruntled former student who lived on a farm or identified with chickens? He had taught many a farm boy over the years, but who would do something like this? Then he remembered Justin Roggerfield, a slow learner who had been very unhappy when Mr. McGregor would not pass him at the end of his eighth-grade year. However, Justin never came back to repeat the grade and didn't seem like one who would be aggressive enough to do a thing such as this. Besides, his folks were too poor to afford to waste a chicken in this manner.

Interrupting his thoughts was a low gurgling sound and movement of the bird on the floor. First there was a twitch of the body, then a jerk of the animal's leg. Mr. McGregor realized immediately that the chicken had only been stunned and was coming to, so he ordered Jim, a farmer's son, to take charge of the poor bird. But Jim didn't want to have anything to do with the victim. He thought the chicken was hexed and would bring him bad luck.

Mr. McGregor was not used to being defied but he recognized that the boy, though big for a seventh grader, was truly frightened for what he imagined could happen to him if he got involved with the chicken. What would have happened next will never be known had Erin not spoken up.

"I'm not afraid of it, Mr. McGregor! I'd like to help the poor chicken!" Erin was only eight but loved all animals and could have cried for the injured fowl. He didn't know how to handle it, but he received suggestions from several farm children in the classroom who told him not to get near the beak or he'd be pecked. In the end, Erin put a big mitten over the chicken's head.

The bird now had regained strength and tried to flap and jump around, but the rock tied to its legs prevented much movement. A piece of glass from the window was still stuck in its upper back. Having cut himself on glass, Erin knew to be careful and very gingerly removed the shard from the bird. More feathers started to fly as the victim then wildly flapped its wings, making Erin back away to avoid them. Blood flowed from the cut so Erin put his arms around the bird, engulfing his wings, putting pressure on the cut and talking to it constantly in low, soothing tones. Luckily, its feet were still tied to the rock, or its claws probably would have scratched Erin.

"Miracle, you're going to be fine. It's all right. I'm going to take good care of you. Quiet down now, Miracle."

The bird seemed to sense the love and care that Erin was offering and after a while calmed down and started to coo in a bubbly manner, as if to thank Erin.

Mr. McGregor was back in charge and ordered a short recess, after which Colleen would read her paper aloud and then there would be the normal Friday Spelldown before dismissal. It wasn't until now, as they put the chicken under a wooden box and took off the cord and rock from around its legs, that Erin noticed something scratched into the bottom of the weight. "Blod be on ya!" He showed the writing to the schoolmaster, whose blood froze and face and hands turned white.

"Erin," said McGregor, "it is not necessary to tell anyone else of this nonsense. Whoever did this is sick. Promise me that you will not spread the contents of this crazy note to your classmates. Say it, boy, say it!"

"I will not tell my classmates about the scratched note on the rock," whispered the now frightened Erin. Then he went outside with the rest of the students.

Chapter 6
THE MYSTERY
Friday, 3 March 1854

"What's the matter with you, Erin?" asked Colleen on their way home after school that day. Erin carried the chicken he had named "Miracle" under his arm with its legs dangling freely. He had won the chicken over with his gentleness, but the curse he couldn't forget. Although he was sworn not to tell his classmates, which included his sister, about the etched threat, it bothered him a lot. Who had thrown the rock with the chicken attached? Who was the threat intended for? Certainly not him, he hoped, but he wasn't sure about any of it. Jim O'Neel had refused to help Miracle for fear that bad luck would follow him. The only thing Erin knew was that he was going to take good care of the chicken, and he gave it a tighter squeeze. The bird gave its bubbly, cooing sound in response.

"I thought you would be so happy to have a pet that you would almost dance all the way home. Here you are, quiet as a mouse . . . and going to get killed if you don't watch out for the horses." A wild-looking fellow on horseback was racing down Madison Street and Erin almost walked in front of him. Colleen held him back.

It was a close call and reminded Erin of the "blod-be-on-ya" danger. "Thank you, Colleen. I'll be more careful." He had to say something as an excuse for his carelessness. "I guess I'm just wondering what Mamma and Papa will say about Miracle."

"Well, if you don't watch out, you won't be around to worry about it!" It was a flippant remark on Colleen's part, but reinforced what Erin was thinking.

Maura was busy preparing supper when the children arrived home. She had her back to them as they entered. Then she heard the clucking of the contented chicken and started to say, "Glory be to God, but that sounds like a – "she turned around – "chicken! Erin, where did you get that animal?" she asked, half-disbelieving her eyes and not wanting it to be true.

"At school, Mamma!" replied the very serious Erin. The two children then told the story of the chicken being thrown through the school window, of people getting cut and needing Mr. McGregor and Colleen's help, of Jim O'Neel refusing to help when the bird started to move, and finally of Erin coming to its assistance.

"Mr. McGregor said I could keep Miracle if it is all right with you and Papa," ended Erin with his eyes intent on his mother.

"Thank the Good Lord that no one was badly hurt! So 'Miracle' it is? Well, that seems appropriate as a name. We'll have to see what your father has to say about keeping it as a pet. Have you thought about what it will eat, where it will sleep, who will take care of it when you are at school? Get washed up now for supper. We'll eat as soon as your father gets home."

Erin had almost forgotten about the threat on the bottom of the rock until he spilled some of the hot water as he poured it into the bowl to wash his hands and face. Then he became quiet again.

Miracle waddled about the house, clucking contentedly and looking for anything on the wooden floor to eat. Maura knew that it could eat the dry oats that she normally cooked for breakfast and also suggested that Erin give it some water in a small bucket. The three of them enjoyed watching Miracle dip its beak into the water and lift its head to swallow.

James arrived home his usual time and opened the door. With the snow from outside blinding him for a moment, he almost stepped on Miracle. They all laughed as Miracle squawked and tried to fly to get out of his way.

"Begorra, what was that?" James exclaimed as Maura went to him for a kiss and hug. After each of the children were greeted likewise, Maura merely said with a flourish, "Papa, meet Miracle!"

Erin told the story again of what had happened at school today, with Colleen inserting a few colorful details. When he finished, he stopped for a breath and asked, "Papa, can I keep Miracle?"

James was fascinated with the children's tale and had seen the question coming. With a twinkle in his eye he answered, "I don't know now if we have the means to keep it. How much of your share of food are you willing to give it?"

"Oh, Papa, the chicken doesn't eat our food! It eats corn, and Mamma gave it some oats it liked. Maybe my farmer friend at school would give me some cobs of seed corn or I could get a job cleaning up the General Store for some feed. I thought he could sleep on the floor next to my bed. What I don't know is who will take care of it all day while I'm at school."

"Glory be, Erin, it appears you have given some thought to its care. Maybe you and I could build a cage for it to stay in when you are gone. I'll see if I can find lumber or an old barrel if nothing else, and this summer maybe you can grow some corn. Until then, I don't think one chicken will send us to the poorhouse."

Erin gave his father a hug around the waist and with tears of relief in his eyes, looked up and said, "Oh, thank you, Papa."

Maura noted that Erin seemed preoccupied all evening. After having achieved a long-time dream of having a pet all his own, Erin should have been ecstatic and talkative, Maura thought. However, that was not so. He ate very little of his supper and did not contribute to the conversation, even about Miracle's comical behavior. The final straw came when, in reaching for his milk, he spilled the whole tin cup. He began to cry and was given permission to leave the table after cleaning it up.

So when the dishes were done and the children were ready for bed, Maura asked Erin what was bothering him. At first he denied having a problem, but not being able to bear it any longer, he said, "Oh, Mamma, I don't want Colleen to hear. Make sure she can't hear." Maura got the screen and put it closer to his bed to give a little more privacy in the close quarters.

"She can't hear now." Maura wasn't so sure that was the case, but it was the best she could do. "What is the matter, Erin?"

"After everyone went out for recess," Erin began, "Mr. McGregor and I untied the cord around Miracle's legs. I picked up the rock, and in handing it to Mr. McGregor, I noticed something scratched onto the bottom. It said, 'Blod be on ya.' I'll never forget it, Mamma."

Erin stopped here and started to cry. Maura hugged him, then he continued, "Mr. McGregor got real white and made me promise I would not tell any of my classmates about the note. That is why Colleen can't hear. He didn't say I couldn't tell you or Papa."

Saying anything in the Kanes' house even in a whisper was like announcing it over a megaphone, and James and Colleen heard almost every word that Erin spoke to his mother. Both parents were aghast but for different reasons. James felt that the schoolmaster should not have sworn such a small boy to secrecy over such a grave matter. Instead, he should have made light of it, assuring Erin that he would take care of it and not to be concerned.

Colleen, on the other hand, had been there and knew nothing of a note. She was worried for the safety of the teacher, for whom she felt great esteem.

No one seemed to understand that Erin felt the jinx was on him for having taken the chicken. He had taken the "Blod be on ya" threat to heart. Hadn't accidents been happening to him ever since he took Miracle? The horse almost ran over him and he had spilled his wash water before supper, followed by his milk at supper.

Only Maura saw the pain in Erin's eyes. "Mamma, I love Miracle and don't want to part with him, but I don't want anything bad to happen to me. Please help me."

"Oh, Erin, nothing bad is going to happen to you! The Good Lord, your father and I will see to that!" she assured him. "The person who threw Miracle through the school window probably doesn't even know you exist. The note has nothing to do with you or Miracle. Miracle was just the sad means of delivering a threat. It appears as though the culprit thought that the chicken would die, and you saved it. Praise be to God! Now you can go to sleep and think only good thoughts of what a good pet Miracle will be." With that Maura gave Erin a hug and a kiss and tucked him in. Erin had taken one end out of a box as a little house for the chicken. However, Miracle preferred being on top of the box, off the floor but beside Erin's bed.

James and Maura were in the habit of having a cup of tea and discussing the events of the day at the kitchen table before going to bed themselves. The candlelight flickered on solemn faces this evening. Few words were spoken until they were sure both children were asleep.

"Maura, we need to talk to Mr. McGregor. He doesn't know what a terrifying impression this has made on Erin. It also might help if he can solve the mystery of who did this cruel deed. He needs to take the weight of this threat off Erin's shoulders. It will continue to be a problem for Erin as long as it is a secret from his classmates."

Maura could not agree more with James. The problem she could see was when they might see the schoolmaster without the children.

That problem was solved the very next day, Saturday, when James and Maura were shopping at the General Store. Mr. McGregor was bending over a barrel of apples.

Maura stood back as James greeted him. "McGregor, thank the dear Lord that we have run into you. I am James Kane and this is my wife, Maura, Erin and Colleen's parents. Just last night we were saying that we needed to talk to you."

The schoolmaster was taken aback by this greeting. Usually people tipped their hats and left him alone, hardly saying anything, possibly feeling a little intimidated because they had little or no education. That was fine with Mr. McGregor, who was a private man and therefore not very social. He knew what it must be about and did not want the subject of the chicken to be broadcast to others. So bowing slightly he responded, "Good day, Mr. and Mrs. Kane! I remember you from the beginning of school. You have two fine children in Erin and Colleen. Yes, we can talk in the schoolhouse, which is only a few blocks away. This is far too public. How will it be if we meet there in an hour?" He bowed again and took several things to the counter to purchase them.

James and Maura were surprised at the rather abrupt meeting with the schoolmaster. He had been rather curt, they felt, but polite. It was plain that he didn't want others to hear. So James found the feed corn and got five cobs for a few pennies. After getting some other staples that they needed, the couple checked out with Mr. Buford, the proprietor.

At 11 a.m. sharp, James and Maura, always prompt, were at the schoolhouse. Mr. McGregor had started a fire in the wood-burning stove but it was still cold in this roomful of desks. They greeted one another, and Mr. McGregor sat on his high stool behind his desk. The Kanes stood rather than sit in the student desks.

James opened the conversation. "McGregor, Erin came home with a chicken yesterday that he says was thrown through a window here at school. That must be the window over there that you have boarded up." James pointed to the covered window, and Mr. McGregor nodded. "Erin was very distraught, upset and couldn't eat well, because he says that you made him swear not to tell his classmates about a note on the rock that was tied to the chicken's legs. It upset him greatly and we are concerned."

With that, James paused and noticed that Mr. McGregor was fidgeting with a ruler on his desk turning it over and over in his hand. His face showed no emotion but its color was a little pale.

"Mr. and Mrs. Kane, Erin is a very sensitive boy, and I did ask him not to reveal the note or its contents to other students. I didn't want to add more trauma to what they had already experienced. I am sorry Erin took it so hard, but I don't know what more I can do."

James was upset. "Glory be to God, McGregor, listen to what you just said: 'I know that Erin is sensitive but I swore him to secrecy to save all the rest from trauma.' You should have told Erin it would be all right, that it had nothing to do with him and may all have been a mistake. You could have said that you would take care of it and that you were sure the person meant nothing by it. Making light of it would have helped him, even saying that maybe we can keep this note a secret until I have a chance to look into it." James said what he wanted to say and was done. He had no ill feelings or animosity toward the schoolmaster.

He knew he had acted under duress, but he wanted him to know the effect it had on Erin.

Mr. Kane, I am sorry. I apologize! Truly I forgot at the time that Erin was only 8 years old and I was treating him like an adult. Even for an adult it would be hard to keep that secret."

"It is to Erin that you need to apologize, not to us. He respects you tremendously and would do almost anything you say."

"Monday I will take care of that. I am sure you have eased his mind for the weekend. Thank you for pointing this out to me."

Maura had been quiet all this time leaving the situation in her husband's capable hands. But now she asked, "Who would do such a cruel thing to the chicken and endanger the lives of the children, as well? Do you have any idea, Mr. McGregor?"

"No! It would have taken a lot of strength to throw both chicken and rock. Not many would have written that phrase. It is a mystery!"

He continued, "Would you like to see the rock?" While opening his desk drawer, the schoolmaster remarked that the window would probably not be replaced this school season. "The parents do not have the money to spend on replacing the glass. As you know, it is costly. I am afraid it is the children that will suffer, with the cold. We may need to wear our coats on windy days the rest of this winter and spring." He had replaced the temporary tin covering with a board that did not fit perfectly and had filled the opening with rags.

Mr. McGregor pulled out a limestone rock from his desk, over six inches in length, along with the cord that had attached it to the chicken. He turned it over to show the Kanes the curse etched in the stone. Maura felt a chill go up her spine when she read the words "Blod be on ya."

"Glory be, but I can almost feel how Erin and you, Mr. McGregor, must have felt reading those words for the first time. It is a real shock! It seems an impossible task, but somehow the one who did this should be found."

James was equally disturbed, but being more of a realist, felt nothing could be done to find the perpetrator. He thanked Mr. McGregor for his time and the couple left the schoolhouse with a more subdued attitude.

Chapter 7
COLLEEN'S PAPER
Monday, 6 March 1854

The weekend was enjoyable for the Kanes. James and Erin together built a chicken house for Miracle that could be moved outside in better weather. It had two levels – the upper for roosting and the lower one for feed and water. It was not very big, but since it was made up of narrow slats with space between, Miracle could see and be seen and it made the structure easier to move.

Watching the chicken from the back waddle around made everyone laugh. James explained that, being a hen, the bird would lay eggs, something that Erin had hoped for.

Miracle and Erin were getting to be a close pair. Erin could pick her up and carry her around, explaining what everything was to her as though she would understand. "This is a table where we eat – but not you – and these are Mamma and Papa's chairs to sit on. This is my stool, but you can sit on it once in a while." When it came to Erin's bed, he was not so generous. But that was all right with Miracle, who clucked the whole time moving her head all around.

By Monday, everyone was quite adjusted to having the fowl in the house and Erin had almost forgotten his fear of something bad happening. When he and Colleen met up with classmates going to school, Erin told them of the funny things that Miracle did. Colleen inquired about the cut on Theresa's arm, which was healing nicely.

Mr. McGregor was in a good mood when they entered the schoolhouse. After the roll call, he declared that he had something he wanted to say. "The incident last Friday is something I would like for all of us to forget. I'm glad to see that Joseph and Theresa's cuts are healing very well. The chicken, which I believe has been named Miracle, has a good home with Erin. The window may not be repaired until summer. The incident is over and we need to concentrate on our schooling. Colleen was about to read her composition before the chicken entered our school." This was the closest thing to a joke that Mr. McGregor had ever made, and the children giggled. He allowed it because of the mood he was in. He continued, "Colleen will read her paper after recess." He then started the reading lesson.

At recess, the schoolmaster asked Erin to stay for a minute. Erin had been feeling fine, but now he worried about what Mr. McGregor would say.

"Erin, I realize now that asking you not to tell about the note scratched into the rock was unfair and unnecessary. Nothing has happened nor will it happen. It was all some kind of prank. You do not need to worry yourself about it anymore."

"Does that mean that I can tell my friends about the note?" Erin asked.

Of course, you may tell them, but it is a real mystery as to who did this evil deed to Miracle. I think it might be better if no more people knew about it. The sheriff or marshal doesn't tell everything to the public when they are solving cases. So why not keep this a secret, for the moment, while you and I try to solve it? The decision is yours."

Erin felt so proud. His teacher was asking him to try to solve this mystery with him. Thoughts were racing through Erin's head. "He said that I could tell my friends about the note. Everyone will be surprised when I tell them. They will want to know what it said – the exact words – and what Mr. McGregor did. But then again, maybe Mr. McGregor is right. Maybe we can find out who did it and then I can tell my friends everything."

"It would be better to keep this secret for now, I guess," was Erin's answer to Mr. McGregor's implied question.

"Good thinking, lad! Now go on out to recess." Mr. McGregor was relieved.

Outside Erin got in the boys' line for the outhouse. By now it was short. Most of the boys were running around playing tag. Brett was Erin's best friend at school and last in line, waiting for Erin to come out. "What did the schoolmaster want, Erin? Are you in trouble? Was it because you threw that spitball at Theresa?"

Erin wasn't sure what to say. "Oh, no, he wants me to work on a special project." Even saying that made him feel important, but he changed the subject by telling Brett about the cage that he and his father had built for Miracle. "We took apart an old barrel. It really looks great. You should come over to see it sometime."

After recess and everyone had settled down, Mr. McGregor asked Colleen to come to the front of the room and read her composition. Somewhat nervously, stepping over boys' feet that were thrust in the aisle in an attempt to trip her, Colleen walked past four rows of desks to the schoolmaster's high table and turned to read. She began and then had to clear her voice so the words would come out. Mr. McGregor kindly said, "Louder, Colleen, so they can hear in back."

"What I Hope My Future Will Bring!" Colleen paused, then continued. "When I grow up, I expect to write stories for a newspaper, read lots of books and marry a wonderful Irishman, like my father. I dream of a door with lighted edges waiting for a grown girl to put her hand on the golden knob, and open the door to a new life. A life where we are not forced to work day after day without a vacation, and make no more than the littlest amount to keep us alive.

"Writing to me is a passion. I would write books and poetry for children to read. I have had fun writing poetry ever since Mr. McGregor introduced us to it last year. This is an example:

> *Life is full of ups and downs.*
> *We experience both, as do clowns.*
> *Ours are mostly ups, we pray.*
> *Clowns turn downs around, they say.*

"Maybe when I'm 18 I'll be ready to meet a man and marry him. He'll have to be kind and friendly, want to help others, be nice-looking, be a hard worker, want children, be adventurous, laugh a lot and be an Irishman. I want to have a family, to wear clothes that others will admire, to hold hands with my family, run in the sand with them and be happy. I want a simple life. This is my future, I believe."

Colleen was red-faced as she walked back to her seat. Everyone was quiet. Mr. McGregor had thought her paper would be an inspiration for others to follow in their writing, but instead, it became a reason to make fun. Big Benjamin, behind the schoolmaster's back, tried to get Colleen's attention and say, "I'm all those things. Will you marry me?"

After school, the boys waited for Colleen just to continue teasing her about her expectations. She wished that she had never read her composition. Erin, by her side, told the boys to leave her alone. The teasing had one good effect in that brother and sister became closer.

Because of this sudden closeness, Erin decided to tell Colleen about the note on the rock and ask for her help in solving the mystery.

Colleen pretended she knew nothing of the written threat of blood, although she actually had overheard Erin when he had told their mother.

"You mean that was written on the rock?" Colleen questioned.

"Words were scratched into the bottom but 'blood' and 'you' were misspelled. Mr. McGregor said not to tell the rest of the class. 'We can solve the mystery together,' he told me at recess. So don't tell any of your friends about the note, Colleen, until after we find out who did it."

"How are you going to do that?" Colleen quizzed. They were still walking home from school, having left all others when they reached the railroad depot area.

"I know what we can do!" responded Erin with confidence.

Chapter 8
THE HUNT
Tuesday, 7 March 1854

Erin, though only 8 years old, had a very logical mind. He had had time to think about the chicken incident and decided they should first look outside the schoolhouse window for evidence. So the next morning, brother and sister left for school a little early. The weather was still bitterly cold so the snow had not melted or changed much since the incident last Friday. The land east of the schoolhouse was kept cropped close for the children to play on and to get to the outhouse, but the area west of the building, near the side road, was high with dried, dead weeds. It was left uncared for all year.

The broken window was on the west side. The Kane children never had occasion to go around there. But this morning they trudged through the snow beside the mostly unused eastern trail to the schoolhouse. A split-rail fence identified where the school grounds ended. There was about 20 feet of space from the road to the building. Being practical, Colleen felt that it was too great a distance for anyone to have thrown the chicken. But getting to the spot underneath the broken window, they noticed that the tall, snowy weeds were trampled down. However, the plants were crushed not from boots, but from horse's hooves. Horseshoe tracks were visible in the snow. They determined that after jumping the fence, the horse had circled several times to give the rider the needed force to throw poor Miracle through the window. There was no glass or wood from the mullions – the wood between the panes of glass – on the ground outside. It had all gone inside.

By this time the schoolmaster was ringing the bell for school to start and Erin and Colleen ran back to Orleans Street and the schoolhouse entrance.

After school that day, the Kane children stayed to talk to Mr. McGregor. He was surprised, because though he had told Erin they could work together on the mystery, he really did not expect an 8-year-old to be of any help. Erin and Colleen told Mr. McGregor what they had discovered that morning.

The schoolmaster first said, "Erin, I thought you were not going to tell anyone, but now I learn you have involved Colleen."

"But, Mr. McGregor," Erin explained, "I only told her so she could help. We have not told anyone else. It is hard for me to do anything without my sister, since we walk to school together. I hope it is all right."

Colleen spoke up. "I will not say anything to anyone, Mr. McGregor. Erin didn't tell me until yesterday after school, and he said you gave him permission."

The schoolmaster was impressed with the integrity of the children, especially Erin, who had held off in telling even his sister until given permission to do so. Mr. McGregor knew Colleen to be responsible. "Then we will be a tight little investigative team. What did you find out so far?"

The children related what they had seen beneath the window. Mr. McGregor again was impressed by the children. He himself had been too busy – with covering the broken window, preparing and grading regular school work and meticulously cleaning up the tiny bits of glass that had covered the room – to look outside. But he had been wracking his brain to think of who might have hated him so much to do such a terrible thing.

"It is interesting to know that the culprit was on horseback. That only makes sense, what with the height of the window. Maybe some of the local merchants saw someone riding with a chicken. It is likely that it would have been covered, but he would not have been able to keep it quiet. See what you can find out. But be discreet so no one will become too curious."

Erin and Colleen were pleased that they could tell Mr. McGregor something that he didn't know. That part had been easy for them to discover. But asking the merchants if they saw the rider was another story. Who would they ask, and when would they have time? This was becoming more complicated all the time.

On their way home that day, they looked around to see which merchants would have been in a position to see anything. Actually, the school was quite isolated. Located on land that was mostly rock and clay, it was not prime farming property and was unwanted for business since it was too far west. Courthouse Square was a block east, and a block beyond that was a carriage and wagon factory. There were no businesses nearby, making the children unsure how to proceed with their investigation.

Colleen had a wild idea. Supposing the person were from out of town and had his horse's hooves shod. Maybe the local blacksmith could tell them something. It was worth a try.

There were two blacksmiths in town and Erin knew where they were. Blacksmith shops were very busy and interesting places for everyone, especially for curious boys. Erin had been there before. However, Erin and Colleen would have to wait until another day to visit because time had passed as they talked and thought, and that it was starting to get dark.

It was Thursday after school before the children were able to visit the first blacksmith shop, almost a week after the chicken had been thrown through the school window. They hoped that the smithy would remember his customers that far back. Mr. Adams – Henry M. Adams – was a big man, probably weighing 250 pounds, tall and very muscular with a thick head of black hair and sideburns to match. He would like to have grown a beard but felt with the constant fire and heat of the shop it would be neither comfortable nor safe.

Coming in from the cold, Erin and Colleen appreciated the heat of the smithy's shop. Immediately they understood why it was so warm. The forge was always going, fed with coal from a supply next to it. Mounted on a log pedestal was an anvil, about six inches wide, on which the blacksmith was hammering hot metal into shape. A large bellows was next to the forge to keep the coals burning. The floor was cobblestone, covered nearly completely with soot. In those few places swept clean by foot traffic, the fire reflected on the cobblestone. The wall was hung with different tools, and horseshoes of every size hung on poles. The room was large enough to accommodate a horse when one needed to be shod. There were narrow windows on three sides and a wide doorway which was sometimes left partially open to equalize the temperature.

The blacksmith was surprised to see the children, especially Colleen. Often boys came to watch the activity, but girls usually had been taught not to get dirty or even to witness the kind of grime that a smithy works with every day. While Colleen had not been taught that kind of genteel behavior and didn't mind the grime, her reasons for being here today were different.

Colleen got right to the point. "Mr. Blacksmith" – she read that on the door and thought that was his name – "We are here on a mission. We hope you can help us. Last Friday morning did you see or maybe shoe a horse for a man carrying a chicken? It may have been covered up in a printed flour sack or newspaper or something."

Mr. Henry Adams smiled at the question. "Young lady, I have so many people coming in here every day that I can't remember them all. As for shoeing a horse, I do maybe eight to twelve a day. I know very few of the owners."

But Colleen wasn't going to give up that easily. "Are you sure that someone with an unusual package didn't come in?"

The blacksmith started to review his last week's customers in his mind. It took a few minutes, but his response was the same. "I never saw anyone with a chicken or a package that could have been a chicken. I'm sorry."

"Thank you, sir." It was Erin this time who spoke up. They were disappointed.

The children were about to go out the large doorway when the blacksmith called to them. "You might ask at the Rock Island House up the road at Illinois and West Eagle. Traveling men often eat there."

Colleen's hopes perked up. She hadn't thought of that, but there were many hotels where people could eat in town. It was worth a try.

Because it was getting late, they would only be able to stop at the one hotel. The Rock Island House was a very prestigious place. They had never been there before and were a little hesitant, but Colleen's determination was greater than her fear. Once she made up her mind to do something, she saw it through.

Erin opened the fancy, etched-glass door with polished gold-colored hardware. It was heavy for him, but he managed. Inside was a lobby in which men were sitting, talking and smoking. The lobby had overstuffed plush furniture and a heavily carved library table with an oil lamp, lit even though it was not dark. Colleen's first glance took in everything. To the right, there was a long counter, behind which a man stood, dressed in a white shirt, black vest and a black cravat around his neck.

The man looked up when they entered. "May I help you?" he asked.

"I'm not sure," began Colleen. "Do you serve breakfast here?"

"Yes, Ma'am, in our dining room." But as a kind of joke he added, "But not at this time." It was about 4 p.m.

It broke the tension for Colleen and she smiled. "Could we speak to someone who works here in the mornings?"

The clerk thought for a moment, "Avery should be able to help you.

Just go through those doors," and he pointed to double doors.

The dining room was filled with tables set for the evening meal. The room was empty until a man dressed all in white came from the kitchen with silverware in his hand. He saw the children and their hesitation and came over to them.

"Is there something I can do for you? My name is Avery."

Colleen hardly knew how to start. This was more elegant than she had expected and may not have been the kind of place the man she was tracing would have chosen. But she was here and she was going to ask.

"Would you have been serving breakfast a week ago? I am looking for a man who traveled on horseback and who would have been carrying a live chicken probably in a flour sack or wrapped in newspaper or something similar, early last Friday." If the girl had not been so serious, Avery would have thought it was a joke. He did not smile but attempted to think of his customers this past week.

"Hmmm, last Friday. Saturday is my day off, so I am feeling pretty good on Friday. A man with a live chicken in a bag. I don't think so. I would remember that I am sure. However, he might have left the package at the desk before coming in. Or he may have had a room here and left it in his room."

Erin spoke up then. "That is great!" Colleen thought it seemed less likely but was willing to ask further. They thanked Avery and hurried back to the registration desk. It was getting late and they needed to start for home soon.

The desk clerk had been intent on some files and looked up when the children returned.

"Did you find Avery?" he asked politely.

"Yes, he was helpful, though he doesn't remember the man we are looking for. He suggested that maybe you might remember him. All we know is that last Friday morning he would have come on horseback and have been carrying a live chicken in a flour sack or wrapped in some way. Do you remember seeing him?" Erin was about in tears from frustration and thinking of his poor Miracle being carried around like that so carelessly.

The clerk noticed Erin's sadness and the seriousness of the girl and refrained from laughing, though it sounded humorous. He knew he would remember anyone like that, but he did try to recall any such person in the hotel last week. It was not uncommon on the street to see people followed by pigs or sheep or other livestock, but in the Rock Island House, that was frowned upon.

"No, I'm afraid I don't," he said. Then he had a second thought. "I do recall one of our overnight guests leaving with a box that did make a sound. I don't know that it was a chicken sound because the box was on the floor when he signed out. Yes, it could have been a chicken," he said.

The children couldn't have been happier. "Can you tell us anything about him? What was his name? What did he look like? Where was he from?" It was almost too good to be true, Colleen thought.

"Slow down, young lady! I will have to look at my records for last Friday." The Rock Island House was well-known in the Midwest. Ever since gold had been found in California, people from the East had flocked to towns along the Mississippi, where they could cross the river by ferry in their muslin-covered wagons. Hundreds came daily, at all hours. Others with more money came by boat down the Ohio and up the Mississippi to Rock Island or Davenport. They would be the ones to stay at the hotel. They were coming daily, so the record books filled quite quickly.

When the clerk retrieved the ledger, he flipped to the last pages and found the proper date. His finger followed the names down the column to the person in Room 257. "Oh, yes! I remember! His name was Alonzo Jones. His home was given as the eastern United States. Strange, isn't it?"

The next morning the sun was finally out and its warmth started to melt the snow. But Colleen and Erin were not thinking about the weather, snow or snowballs today. They couldn't wait to tell Mr. McGregor the exciting news: that they had the name of the perpetrator of that evil deed, the name of the person who hurt some of their classmates and almost killed Miracle.

They had no time before school but had to wait until recess. Erin was beside himself with excitement. He was sure that the schoolmaster would congratulate them and be pleased to have solved the mystery. He could then tell his friends what really happened and who did it. But that was not to happen.

"Alonzo Jones?" Mr. McGregor's face turned red at first, then white the more he thought about the name. Finally his face took on an almost twisted look of hate and fear. But he told the children nothing.

"Mr. McGregor! Mr. McGregor! Can we tell our friends about the note now and who threw the rock?" asked Erin. He was beginning to worry about his teacher. He had never seen anyone change so completely in appearance in such a short time. He hardly looked like the person they saw every day.

"No, do not tell anyone anything. I'll have to take care of this myself," Mr. McGregor almost whispered through a tight mouth. Erin and Colleen learned no more, but the rest of the day Mr. McGregor acted strangely. For the first time in his 18 years of teaching, he was distracted, fumbling, unfocused. Yet, he had a look about him that let the children know they had better not try anything out of line today.

Maura was full of questions when Erin and Colleen arrived home after school that afternoon. The children had spent so much of their time after school trying to solve this mystery. She thought it was now over and things could go back to normal. Well, maybe not normal, exactly, because Miracle was now a part of their life.

"What did Mr. McGregor say when you told him the name of the man who threw the chicken through the school window? Did he recognize the person . . . Alonzo Jones? What kind of a grudge did he have with him?"

"But, before you answer, Erin, you had better take care of Miracle. She is squawking so loud I can hardly hear anything anyway. She wants out of that pen. Get her some more water and food in her pails and clean out the cage." Most of this work had been left up to Maura while the children were doing their investigating, but Erin was Miracle's true friend and master, and the chicken was trying her best to let Erin know how glad she was to see him.

Erin immediately went to the cage and got Miracle out. He petted the chicken and it squatted down, ready for Erin to pick it up. When Erin did this, Miracle's tone became like a bubbling, cooing sound of satisfaction. A great bond had formed between the two.

As Erin put her down and filled Miracle's bowl with a mixture of corn, oatmeal and sand, Colleen, who had been watching her brother and Miracle, answered her mother. "Mamma, Mr. McGregor recognized the name, but he didn't say anything for a while. His appearance and color turned from normal to red to ashen." Ashen was a word she had recently discovered and it seemed to fit. "He could hardly talk he was so upset. It seemed to be both anger and fear. When Erin asked if we could now tell our friends about the note and who threw it, his answer was 'No!' He looked so mean and ugly that we didn't want to ask him more. So we went outside to recess."

Maura was standing as if in shock. "What is there in Mr. McGregor's past that is causing such a reaction?" she thought. The children have done all they can to solve this mystery and now it has come back to McGregor himself.

"God willing, in the fullness of time we may find out what the reason was for Alonzo Jones's actions, but you have done all you can do. So it is best if you can forget it. Sometimes things like this happen and we never find out why." That is what Maura said, but not what she planned for herself. She and James would see what they could find out about this Alonzo Jones and John McGregor. She was too curious to drop it. But for now, it was time to get supper.

Chapter 9
THE GANNONS
Sunday, 12 March 1854

It was Sunday and the Kanes went out for Mass. Colleen was pleased to see Tom Gannon coming. She had hoped he might be there, but she was so intent on watching him, that she didn't notice a large rock that had fallen in her path from a passing wagon, partially hidden by snow. She hit it with her high-top boot and it threw her off balance. Down she went in the partially snow-covered dirt street, sprawled out flat. It caused a little commotion and she tore the bottom of her new dress that Mamma had made her. Embarrassed, red-faced and covered with dirty snow, she was helped up by her father. As she was brushing herself off, young Gannon ran over to see if he could help. "Are you all right?" he said slightly out of breath. "My name is Tom Gannon. I noticed that you had an accident and thought you might be hurt. Can I help you?"

"What a way to meet him," Colleen thought, but outloud she assured him that she was fine. He gently took her arm the rest of the way into church. Then he nodded slightly and went to sit with his family. Colleen's heart was all aflutter.

Erin thought all the attention his sister was getting was crazy. "After all, she only fell down. It isn't like she was hurt." He was a little jealous, since he was the one who usually had a fuss made over him. To him, girls were to be avoided since they were the ones who got him and his friends in trouble. Tom's actions were a puzzle to him.

On leaving the church, the Gannons met up with the Kanes. The adults exchanged niceties and inquired as to Colleen's health. Tom offered her a ride home in their buggy rather than having her walk "with a possible injury." There was no room for the whole family, so only Colleen and Erin rode.

It was the first time they had ever had the opportunity to even see inside a carriage, let alone ride in one. It was full, with the three little Gannons on one side and Tom, Erin and Colleen on the other, with Tom holding the littlest one on his lap. Mr. and Mrs. Gannon sat above. Tom introduced his siblings, all boys – John, age 4, Patrick, age 5, Sean, age 10, and Frankie, age 2, on his lap. The boys started poking one another and laughing, just a little embarrassed with the company. But Erin, not being bashful, started a conversation with Sean, who was closest to his age. They were not in the same school since the Gannons lived in

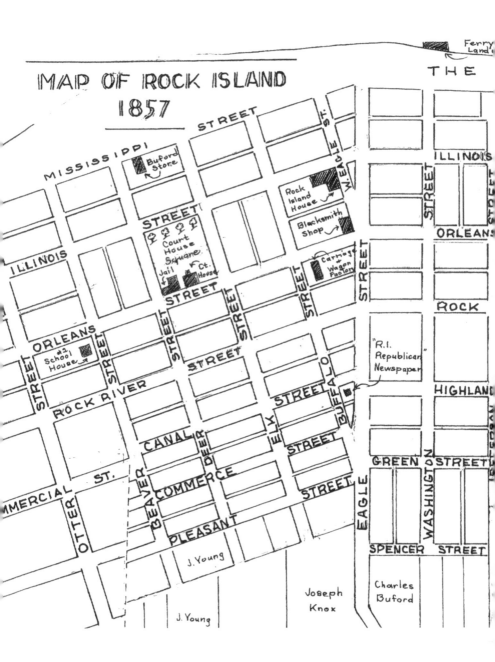

MAP OF ROCK ISLAND 1857

48

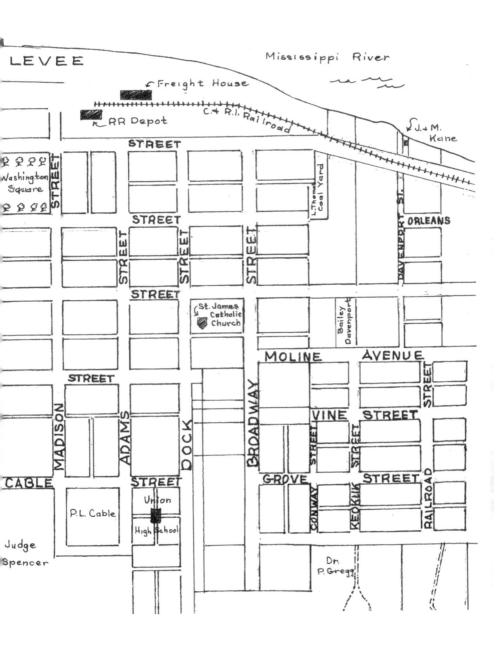

LEVEE

Mississippi River

Freight House

RR Depot

C. & R.I. Railroad

J. & M. Kane

STREET

Washington Square

STREET

STREET

L. Thomas Coal Yard

STREET

STREET

STREET

DAVENPORT ST.

ORLEANS

STREET

STREET

St. James Catholic Church

Bailey Davenport

MOLINE

AVENUE

STREET

STREET

BROADWAY

VINE

STREET

MADISON

ADAMS

DOCK

STREET

STREET

CONWAY

KEOKUK STREET

RAILROAD

CABLE

GROVE

STREET

P.L. Cable

Union High School

Judge Spencer

Dr. P. Gregg

49

Moline, but they got along well, talking about marbles, trains and school.

Colleen asked Tom what he did. He said he was a scholar in high school in Moline, but he also worked for *The Republican* newspaper in Rock Island evenings and would be fulltime this summer. Colleen was intrigued. He told her that he just set type. "However, it is an exciting place to be because with telegraph lines finished just last year, we get the news from New York, Chicago and other places out east all the time. I know the news first. They are training me the business from ground up and eventually I will be a reporter."

Colleen's blue eyes were sparkling and huge, totally focused on her new friend. All thoughts about her fall and any embarrassment were gone. What Tom was doing sounded so exciting. Her mind was racing with ideas. What if he could get her a job there? She would love to be a reporter or a writer in some fashion for the newspaper.

Tom saw the glint in Colleen's eyes and he was encouraged to continue. "With all the talk about the bridge going up and resentment by the steamboat people in our area and in St. Louis, the next few years are going to be very interesting. Did you know that right now there are 'Stop the Bridge' clubs in New Orleans and St. Louis?"

Colleen only had time to say she had never heard such a thing when their conversation was interrupted. They had arrived at the Kanes' humble abode. Mr. Gannon had taken a roundabout way home so that Erin and Colleen could enjoy the experience and get acquainted with his children. By now James and Maura had been home for a while, having walked fast.

When all the goodbyes were said and the Gannons' buggy was gone, the two children could not be quieted from telling about their new friends. It had been a truly good morning.

Chapter 10
MYSTERY SOLVED
Monday, 20 March 1854

Maura couldn't get the events of the last few weeks out of her mind – the chicken incident at school, the mysterious threat to Mr. McGregor, the children spending all their free time to find out who had done the horrible deed, and now Mr. McGregor's angry reaction to the name of the perpetrator, as well as his refusal to disclose the reason or let the children have closure and peace.

"James, God willing, you and I must solve what is going on with the schoolmaster and Alonzo Jones."

James wasn't so sure they should get involved, but he did agree the children deserved a better answer from Mr. McGregor. "But what can we do? We don't know his past. He's been here teaching forever, it seems. Maura, I think this is impossible."

However, Maura would not be swayed. "Nothing is impossible with God's help," she replied firmly, as her Irish background always taught her. She already had a plan. Going to Mr. McGregor would do no good, she knew, but the Rock Island School Board should have the record of his hiring in 1836.

The next day Maura put on her next-best dress and her warm cape and boots and walked into town to see Mr. Buford. He was on the school board and might help, she felt.

His store was empty of customers on this midweek late morning, for which she was grateful. After exchanging general weather and family health queries, Maura came right out and asked, "Mr. Buford, does the school board have a record of the schoolmaster's background, like where he came from or where he went to college?"

A little surprised at the pointed questions about their well-thought-of and respected master, Mr. Buford responded, "Mrs. Kane, our records at hiring John McGregor are so old that I don't know where they would be. It is no secret though that he came from the Boston area. What college or teacher training school he attended, I don't know. Why this sudden interest, may I ask?"

Maura didn't want to reveal her real reason for the questions, so she just said that Colleen was growing up fast and was thinking of becoming a teacher, all of which was true. "I just wondered where Mr. McGregor got his excellent training."

51

"Why don't you ask him?" was Mr. Buford's response.

"Really, I don't want to put more pressure on Colleen by letting him know." She had to come up with some reason in a hurry and that was all she could think of.

"McGregor comes into the store all the time. Maybe I can find out for you, Mrs. Kane. I won't let him know who asked."

A little disappointed that she didn't find out more, Maura bought some honey and left the store. She didn't want it to look like all she wanted was the information. To her surprise, she met Tom Gannon as she was headed down the boardwalk. She thought he should be in school and she said as much.

"Classes were canceled today because of a teacher's conference. How is everything at the Kane residence?" he asked.

After a little conversation, Tom said that he was getting something at the general store before going to the newspaper office. Maura thought maybe Tom might help find out about Mr. McGregor's past through the newspaper's telegraph.

"I'm sorry, Mrs. Kane. We can't run personal messages through the telegraph, but we have an employee who came from the east. Did you say he was from the Boston area?" Maura nodded in agreement. "Hector is from there also. Hector Jumper is his name. I'll ask him if he knows McGregor or his family. I'll let you know. Is it all right to tell Colleen if I see her?"

"No, Tom, I don't want her or Erin to worry any more about the chicken mystery. You do know what happened, don't you?"

When Tom said "No" to the question, Maura proceeded to tell him the story in shortened form. "Someone threw a bewitched note on a rock and a live chicken through the school window. Some of the children were hurt by the flying glass, though not badly. Colleen and Erin found out who did the dastardly deed, but Mr. McGregor has some hidden connection to Alonzo Jones that will not let him explain why. Our children are vowed to secrecy for life, it appears, because of it. The only good thing that has come out of it is 'Miracle,' the chicken, who is now Erin's pet. Now I would like to find out the reason to clear it all up, without the children knowing as yet."

Tom agreed that he would only tell Maura any discovery he made about Mr. McGregor, if any.

That very day Tom saw Hector. He was a short, 50-ish man, with a kind, round face. He always spoke to Tom and Tom liked him. Today after his greeting, Tom asked, "Hector, I believe you told me that you came from Boston. Is that true?"

The man stopped what he was doing at his desk and said, "That is correct, Tom."

"I was wondering if you might have known or heard of an Alonzo Jones or a John McGregor from Boston when you were there?"

"You know, I've been gone from Boston for fifteen years. I don't recall the first name ... Alonzo Jones, was it? But there was a McGregor name in the news. I didn't know him but it was something about his wife. I remember he was a young college graduate, newly married, the newspapers said. His young wife was found dead of an unknown cause. There was a much-publicized bitter trial because the woman was the mayor of Boston's daughter. McGregor was found innocent, but many people still felt he poisoned her. Later it came out that she had a weak heart. McGregor's life was threatened by others, the newspapers said, so he left the area. That affair is what got me interested in writing and reporting. Probably that is why I am here. I could see the importance of good reporting. What is your interest, Tom? Do you know the fellow? Is he in Rock Island?"

"No, I don't know him. A friend asked me to inquire. If it is the same person, he is in town. But there may be many John McGregors in the country. Thank you for your help, Hector."

Tom made it a point to go see Maura at home to tell her what he had discovered. "Alonzo Jones may have been anyone from the East who thought McGregor got away with murder. Or he could have been closer to the situation or the couple than we know. It makes no difference. The strange death of McGregor's wife, at least we can assume, was the cause of the chicken incident and the reason why McGregor didn't want it all brought up again. It seems you can let it rest."

Maura agreed aloud, but not in her heart.

Chapter 11
CALICO ROAD
Tuesday, 28 March 1854

Maura and James were very happy with life. Things were working out – Miracle was fitting in with her pampered houselife, the children had settled down and James had a steady job. "God is good!" said Maura. However, James was traveling farther and farther each day as the track moved out of Davenport. His men worked hard – first leveling the ground, then preparing the bed of crushed rock, lifting the heavy ties into place about six inches apart and finally spiking the rails to them. James had a great relationship with his men, many of whom also were Irish. He knew their names and about their families and so would inquire about their loved ones. Being a compassionate person, James could understand them and could feel for them in their problems and laugh with their joys. Besides, not long ago he was a young worker himself, eager to feed his family.

Things were going along very well until one cold but sunny Spring day when Mr. Glenn Carmichael, general contractor for the M&M Railroad, sent for James. The meeting place was a small shanty in the village of Durant, Iowa, about halfway along the line the track would take to Iowa City. Most of the land was flat, but was overgrown with lots of prairie grass, some as high as 10 to 12 feet, that the men had to cut down as the track snaked its way toward Iowa City.

It was late morning when the two men arrived – Carmichael on horseback and James on the crew's horse and wagon. Mr. Carmichael had not met with him before like this so James was concerned. What could he have in mind? James knew the work he and his men had been doing was unquestionable. Perhaps it was to congratulate him? But, no, he would not take work-time to do that. Mr. Carmichael looked very serious when they both dismounted and entered the shed. There was only a table scattered with papers and a large hand-drawn map and two chairs inside. They shook hands and sat down.

"Kane, I want you to know that the board of the M&M Railroad is very pleased with your work. The track is moving along according to schedule. My reason for calling you here has to do with your pay," he began. "Since our corporation was formed and the ground-breaking held last September 1st, we have had many expenses and at this point have depleted our backlog. Money is in short supply, as you well know. Many people are going into debt, buying land from the government, and are bartering for almost everything else. They are not able to invest in our venture. The bridge is a year away from completion, according to the plan, and people are not able to see beyond that. So what I am saying to you is that, although we don't have the money, we do have access to bolts and bolts of dry goods – calico, to be exact – and we would like the men to take that in partial payment for work. In addition, we have stores and can provide some food items. What do you think? Would they be willing to work for dry goods and food as payment?"

James was stunned as Carmichael finished speaking. He had not anticipated this! How would his men take this news of payment not in dollars but in calico and food? He knew how he felt – like someone had just pulled the rug out from under him. No more paychecks? How would he – or his men – be able to provide for their families with calico and a little food?

Mr. Carmichael saw the dismay on James's face and said, "Go back and tell your men and let me know. The only alternative is to stop work altogether." With that, Carmichael held the shed door open and James left.

James didn't tell the crew when he returned because he had to figure out first what he himself wanted to do. It was not that there was any choice. It was a great blow – not only for himself, but for his crew of good Irishmen with families. He felt responsible because he was their leader. There might be other jobs out there, but for what pay? The economy was slow and money almost nonexistent...but calico? He would first talk it over with Maura.

When he arrived home from work that evening, it was late because he had given the other men a ride in the horse-drawn wagon to the Davenport shoreline as usual. Then he had taken the ferry across the river to Rock Island and walked the short distance home. Maura was waiting for him in a clean apron and freshly brushed hair. The children came up for their usual greeting of hugs and kisses. Erin was getting a little big for a "swing-around" and James didn't feel much like it tonight either.

Supper was cabbage, potatoes and beef brisket and then it was bedtime for the children. James suggested that he and Maura go for a walk. The moonlight, reflected on the river, was beautiful but James hardly noticed it.

"Maura, we have some big decisions to make," he started. He explained what Patrick Carmichael had told him this morning. In their thirteen-year marriage they had always talked things out, making problems seem only half as bad. But this time he wasn't sure that sharing would split this calico headache.

Maura listened intently, then exclaimed, "Glory be to God, James! You still have work. It is not the end of the world. I can use the calico for making curtains, dresses and even shirts for you and Erin. I'm sure the general store would exchange it for our simple needs. Take the offer and encourage your men to do so. We'll be all right!" Secretly she was not so sure, but she knew she had to be positive for her husband's sake.

Her practical attitude surely lifted a great weight from James. He began to think maybe he could sleep tonight after all.

Erin and toy horse on "his" mountain

Chapter 12
NEWSPAPER
Thursday, 30 March 1854

Progress on the Slough Bridge continued. As soon as the ice had left the Mississippi River in the spring of 1854, the workmen began on the superstructure, first building the falsework or scaffolding to support the beams and trusses until they could support themselves on the piers. This work, done above water, was fascinating to Erin. He dressed in his warmest clothes because the late March winds were cutting, even though the sun beat down on his private mountain of dirt. He brought along a little carved toy horse his father made for him, named Chester, and made trails for it with sticks and barriers of dirt for it to jump over. This kept him occupied while watching the bridgework.

One day as a team of horses hauled a huge beam toward the bridge site, a chain broke and the log fell, causing a big thump and dirt to fly. Luckily, the man below jumped out of the way. This accident frightened Erin, though he was safe on his hill. "Remember, the horses will not look out for you" was always his father's warning. Of course, he had been forbidden from going anywhere close to the bridge, a rule for which he was grateful that day.

The *Rock Island Republican* newspaper office was about a mile away from Colleen's house, but she had never really paid attention to it before. Now, however, she was most interested. The Kanes did not have the money to buy the daily paper, but at school the schoolmaster felt it was a good learning tool, so it was always in a rack for extra reading. Now Colleen wished that it wasn't summer vacation so she could read the articles that Tom had set. Of course, she would have no idea on which ones he actually had worked. She even decided she would ask Mr. McGregor for the old newspapers sometimes with the excuse of using them for gift-wrapping or for making dress patterns.

Today was Monday, washday in most homes, and the Kanes' was no exception. Maura filled a large iron kettle of water from the cistern and put it above the coals in the fireplace to heat. She poured that hot water into a large, oval-shaped copper washtub partially filled with cold water. Shaved lye soap and a scrub-board lay close by. Today she washed

Colleen's new dress, the one that had gotten dirty with her fall on the street. She had already mended the torn bottom. She gently rubbed the soapy dress between her hands. The stains came out easily. Maura was grateful for that since she had invested a lot of love and time in making it for her daughter. It was some of the calico that James had earned.

Colleen was more talkative than usual. "Mamma, are you going to the general store today?" she asked. "I can do that for you!" she offered.

Maura was taken by surprise. On washday Colleen was a big help, lifting the hot-water containers and helping hang the sheets on the outdoor clothesline, even in winter. But she had never offered to do any shopping. "It appears she is growing up," Maura pondered. Out loud she said, "There are some things we need! Glory be to God, do you think you can do that for me? After washing all morning, I am tired and would be happy not to have to walk into town." She said, "Yes, dear, that would be very good. I'll write down what we need."

Colleen could hardly contain herself. She planned to get the supplies and then go by the newspaper office and see if she might see Tom Gannon. She started getting ready by putting on the next-best dress she owned, since the best one was on the clothesline. She brushed her long black hair 50 times before braiding it and then pinning it up on top of her head like her mother did sometimes. That way Colleen was sure she looked older. She had a small, white bonnet her mother had made for her of crinoline and ribbons. Her good shoes were rather tight on her feet so she thought she would walk barefooted until she got to the store and then put them on. The weather had turned unusually warm for April. No one would know because her long skirt and petticoats would hide her feet anyway. That way she would be more comfortable and could save her shoes from wear on the cobblestone and boardwalks in town.

She had no trouble getting to Buford's General Store and Mr. Buford recognized her after a second glance. "You are alone today, Colleen?" he said. "My, how grownup you look! What can I do for you?"

Colleen gave him her mother's list. While he was getting the supplies, she looked around at the fabric, ribbon and patterns that were on one side of the store opposite the foodstuffs. She liked to dream of the beautiful dresses she might have someday and the places she might wear them.

Mr. Buford interrupted her thoughts. "Everything is here, Colleen. I bundled everything so you can carry them easier and will bill them to your father's account. Say hello to him for me."

Almost before he was finished speaking, Colleen was out the door, her package in her arm and her shoes on her feet. She only had a few more blocks to go to the newspaper office. She hurried, feeling very anxious because she wasn't sure what she would do once there. The boardwalks and dirt streets weren't very level, making her tight shoes still more uncomfortable. She saw on the side of the two-story brick building the words *The Rock Island Republican*. The building had glass display windows in front with yesterday's feature story displayed, "Grand Excursion Set for June." The subtitle read, "Can Railroads and Riverboats Cooperate?"

Inside was a counter but no person was in sight. Colleen waited a minute. What should she do? Tom would be in the back or upstairs, she was sure. She had an idea. Then an older woman appeared from the back room.

"I was wondering if you needed any help? I love to write and I read everything I can get my hands on. A friend of mine, Tom Gannon, works here. Do you have any openings?"

The woman looked at Colleen and smiled. "How old are you, young lady?" she asked. Colleen hesitated. She hadn't counted on this. "Thirteen...plus!" she answered.

"We don't hire women!" was her response. "Women can't even vote, let alone hire out."

Colleen responded in surprise, "But you're a woman!"

"I am the publisher's wife," the woman explained. "Money is hard to come by in these times. So I help out. But we do not ordinarily hire women." She continued, "But would you like to see your friend?"

"Yes, please!" was Colleen's relieved answer. She knew her parents wouldn't let her work even if the woman said yes. It took a while for Tom to appear. He had a black leather apron on hanging from his neck and tied behind his back, his hands were dirty from handling the lead type, and his forehead had beads of perspiration from the hot quarters in which he worked. His surprise at seeing Colleen was obvious but his pleasure was equally visible.

"Colleen, what an unexpected pleasure!" he exclaimed with a large grin on his face. "How are you?" he added, thinking of her fall on Sunday.

Colleen by now was wondering what she was going to say to him. She had not thought this far ahead and knew that well-brought-up ladies are not usually so forward. But she was here now and needed to make the best of it.

"Mamma wanted me to buy some supplies at Buford's General Store, so I thought I would come to see the newspaper office you said was so exciting." That was the best she could come up with at the moment but now wished she had not come. "I'll be going, now. Thank you." She turned toward the door.

"Come back, Colleen," Tom cried out. "You can't go without seeing how the newspaper is printed!" Since his right hand was dirty from having set type, Tom was careful to offer his left hand to escort her through the inner door to the newsroom. Two of his colleagues were in the newsroom: one was an older man at a desk, whom he introduced to her as the owner/publisher. "This is my friend Colleen Kane, who is a writer and wants to know more about our newspaper's workings."

Mike Farrell extended his hand to her and warmly added, "We're always glad to have the local citizens drop in for a tour, Miss Kane. Tom, show her around."

Colleen smiled to herself. She felt so mature at that moment. Mike Farrell had called her "Miss Kane." She was so glad she had worn her bonnet and had put her braids on top of her head.

The other person was a reporter, probably her father's age, writing something and watching a paper come in with type on it. Tom said this was the telegraph machine and news was coming from New York. Reading over the reporter's shoulder, she saw, "Stagecoach Robberies Increase."

From here they went up the stairs to the pressroom where Tom worked. His area was an arm-high table covered with a tray of different carved alphabets with heavy metal backing. He used these to compose the copy. After Tom put the letters of the story on a story board, the editor, to whom she was introduced, laid out pages and headings, with the date and *Rock Island Republican* banner above. This would be inked and printed.

"The advertising pages are more interesting to see because of the drawings of a plow or piano or whatever is being sold," commented Tom. "We just 'put the newspaper to bed.' The noise you hear is the press printing today's paper. That is why I have time to talk to you now, Colleen." Tom pointed to the big black machine in the other half of the upstairs. It is always busy and bustling but usually not so noisy up here until they start the presses. They'll be on the street soon."

By now Colleen was aware of the time and was anxious to leave, knowing that her mother would be worried. She thanked Tom for the tour and left in rather a hurry. She removed her shoes and clutched her bundle of purchases and ran as best she could after leaving the downtown area.

"Heavenly days, child, where have you been? I've been beside myself with worry that something had happened to you," began her mother as Colleen came in breathless, bonnet askew, black hair and face glistening with perspiration.

Colleen had never lied to her mother, so she told her everything, but played down the reason for going to the newspaper in the first place. "I just wanted to see where the newspaper was and what it was like inside." She didn't elaborate on her applying for work or asking to see Tom. "Tom came and showed me around. Mamma, it was thrilling to see the news come in on the telegraph machine all the way from New York. The press was big, black, complicated and noisy. I am sorry I made you worry."

Maura was glad to know what had delayed her daughter and could tell there was a little puppy love going on. She chided Colleen for not having told her what she really had planned when Colleen had volunteered to do the shopping.

That evening, Maura told James, "We'll have to keep a closer eye on Colleen. You should have seen her today...all dressed up with her braids up, bonnet on and cheeks aglow. James, I think our daughter is smitten with Tom Gannon."

Chapter 13
ANTI-CLIMAX
Wednesday, 12 April 1854

Miracle was a busy chicken. She liked pecking on Erin's bed covers in the early morning and would then moved around the room looking for bugs and crumbs. Maura called her "the broom." Erin was responsible for finding the little messes Miracle left behind.

Now that the weather was warm and the days longer, Erin and James had built a fenced area outside. Miracle could enjoy the fresh air rather than being in a cage during the day. Free to peck and dig, she was growing fat.

The barrel-coop that James had built her for inside had been moved outside where it kept away the elements. At night, she would crouch in a corner of her pen to sleep.

Miracle enjoyed the freedom to move around the yard and peck at the small rocks and seeds she could find there. However, the passing trains with their whistles on one side of the yard and the boat horns on the other side scared her at first. She would get frantic and run in the opposite direction, flapping her wings in an attempt to fly, but would get up only a foot or so off the ground. Coming down, she would run another five feet and try to fly again. It was to no avail. There was no way to get away, and eventually she got used to the sounds.

Several weeks had passed since the chicken-throwing mystery seemed to have been resolved by Tom Gannon and Maura. Then, one day at school, the drama re-emerged. Mr. McGregor was just finishing the reading lesson for the day when the door to the schoolhouse burst open and a clean-shaven, middle-aged man stood in the doorway. His dress was that of a gentleman – with a double-breasted swallow-tailed coat, grey striped pantaloons, and high-collared shirt with a soft silk bow tie and a silk top hat – but his facial expression was that of a rogue, twisted and mean.

Mr. McGregor turned with his mouth open ready to reprimand whomever opened the door in that way, but he froze to the spot when he saw who it was.

"Murderer! Murderer! You are free, while my sister lies rotting in her grave. I hate you and want to make your life miserable," yelled the intruder.

The schoolmaster gained his composure and, knowing that he had to take care of his students safety first, calmly said, "Alonzo, come in and close the door. Class, we will have a recess now. Get your coats on and go outside!"

The students did as they were told and in a minute the room was cleared, all but for Erin and Colleen.

"Colleen and Erin, do as I say!" said the irritated McGregor.

But the two children knew who this was, and there were not about to leave. "We are not going," said Colleen firmly. "This man has already threatened your life when he tied the chicken to the rock and threw it in the window."

"I was not aiming to hurt anyone, only to scare John McGregor," retorted Alonzo Jones. "He has made my life a hell on earth. He poisoned my sister, who was so...kind, gentle, caring, young and beautiful." The man's face softened and he was almost in tears as he talked about his sister. "After my parents died, I decided to hunt him down. It took a while, but now that I have found him, I want to make him pay for what he did."

"You are all wrong, Alonzo," said Mr. McGregor, his voice barely audible. "Angela was all that you say and more. I suffered terribly at her death. She was my companion, my lover, my helpmate, and my best friend. We had only been married a short time, but we had planned to have a family and to have a long, happy life together."

Mr. McGregor had to clear his throat in order to go on. "I didn't poison Angela! She became ill unexpectedly. The doctor said that she had a weak heart. Her death was a terrible blow to me. After the trial, at which the jury found me innocent, I left the Boston area to start over. It was unbearable for me to stay there, as many people still thought me guilty. I moved here to Rock Island. And, since I couldn't have a family of my own, at least I could be near children by teaching." He paused, "I felt that Angela would approve of that."

Erin chimed in, "If Mr. McGregor says he didn't do it, he didn't do it. He always teaches us to be honest. He wouldn't let any of us get by with lying. And he teaches us to always do the right thing. He couldn't do anything bad like that. When Joseph and Theresa were hurt by the broken glass, he made sure they were treated right away. He was even concerned about the chicken being hurt and not having a home. He is always thinking of others. No, Mr. McGregor could not poison anyone."

Erin was so matter-of-fact and positive that Alonzo's attitude started to change.

"Well, if that is true, I have wasted a lot of time and energy accusing and hating him," the man said. He grew very quiet.

There was a long pause while Alonzo reflected on what both McGregor and Erin had just related. The room was hushed as he reconsidered his feelings of revenge toward his former brother-in-law.

Finally, he said, "McGregor, I never got to talk to you after my sister died. It just happened so fast. And then my parents were sick. I guess I blamed everything on you. Angela would not want me to hurt the one she loved without proof. If the children believe in you so sincerely, I guess maybe I was wrong. I apologize for my actions, John. I don't know what else I can do to make up for my actions."

"I know! You can come to see my chicken, Miracle," said Erin.

Everyone laughed. The high tension that had built up in the room was gone. Alonzo and John shook hands and Alonzo left.

Later, at a special meeting for the parents and children, Mr. McGregor told his story. He had been afraid he would lose his position as teacher because of the original trial, as well as Alonzo's accusations and threats that the children had brought home with them. But the school board and parents, grateful for all that the schoolmaster had done for their children over the past 18 years, not only kept him on but also gave him a raise.

"Hoorah for Mr. McGregor," cheered all the children at school the next day.

Chapter 14
GRAND EXCURSION
Monday, 5 June 1854

June 5th was a giant day for all Rock Islanders. For a week the civic leaders had been sprucing up the town. Street lamps were strung with red, white and blue buntings, buildings used for business and some private homes displayed flags, but mostly the riverbank had a lot of activity. Steamboats lined the levee – seven of them, Erin counted – and they, too, were all decorated.

Erin and Colleen were both thrilled. Former President Millard Fillmore, Charles Dana of *The New York Sun*, historian George Bancroft and the governor of Illinois were coming from Chicago by special train. Hundreds of others were slated to fill the train to re-enact the celebration which had started in February. The "marriage" of the Atlantic Ocean and the Mississippi River, as it has been so designated in *The Rock Island Republican*, was too great an event to end with one day. Now that it was June and the river was open to navigation, the steamboats became involved and were going to take the celebrities, visitors and locals alike from Rock Island to the Falls of St. Anthony in Minnesota, head of navigation on the Mississippi River.

It was Monday, the beginning of the week, and everyone in town, plus hundreds from around the country, were enjoying the festivities. The hotels were full and private citizens were even asked to accommodate the overflow. It had been highly advertised as "a Grand Excursion" and the response was so great, with so many people who had not been invited or expected that the original five boats were not enough. Two more boats – the *Jenny Lind* and the *Black Hawk* – were added. The reception for this train was larger and more festive than that for the first train in February, the difference being that now the riverboat people were also a part of the festivities. Today, the steamboats were displaying their prowess.

Erin couldn't wait! He was ready to race to the depot at the crack of dawn.

"Hurry, Colleen, we don't want to be late. People are lined up all along the tracks, almost outside our door. But I want to be at the depot when the train arrives, see the President and see the big steamboats leave." He thought his sister was ready, then she thought of something else she needed – a parasol.

"It is going to be hot out there," she said as she delicately pulled the elongated package wrapped in cloth from under her bed. It had been a gift for her thirteenth birthday that she cherished. This was her first opportunity to use it.

"Colleen!" Erin screamed, exasperated. "Let's go!"

People were lining the tracks for blocks, as Erin said, but the crowds were harder to get through nearer the depot and the grandstand. The children saw friends from school and church, but it took them a while to find their parents. The organizers had reserved seats for special people involved with the event. James Kane was one of them. But even so, the adult Kanes had arrived early to insure their places would not be taken.

James and Maura were in their best clothes, their "Sunday-go-meetin'" clothes, as James would say. Maura's was a flowery, fitted-bodice dress with full, long skirt held out with many petticoats, but no bustle, as was popular with the more elite. Her straw bonnet was one she had done over other years, but matching dress material and ribbon made it look new. A light green shawl covered her shoulders to protect her from the river breezes of early June.

James' shirt had the typical high stand-up collar, narrow crossed and buttoned tie, and three-buttoned coat that almost matched his now thread-bare pantaloons. New pants were not a high priority for him, now that his pay was minimal. Maura hoped they could afford new clothes soon.

The train announced itself with a loud whistle. Bells rang out, the band played loudly and the excitement of the crowd escalated. Erin and Colleen squeezed in next to their folks. Everyone stood to see the now familiar rolling cloud of smoke coming from the bulbous smokestack. The train – decorated with red, white and blue flowers, flags and streamers – came to a standstill as the lineup of steamboats in the river gave a unanimous whistle welcome and a cannon was shot off in the distance. It was just 4 p.m.

Within minutes the dignitaries deboarded. The first was former President Fillmore (1850-1853), then Senator Dix of Iowa, and Judge Grant, Mayor of Davenport. People gave a rousing applause as they and many other officials took their seats. Among them were Henry Farnam and Joseph E. Sheffield, who were the original contractors for the construction of the Chicago and Rock Island Railroad.

When the band had played its last note, the people in the stands sat and the ceremonies began. Everyone on the stage had a brief message about this joyous occasion – the grand excursion by steamboat to the Falls of St. Anthony, in Minneapolis, Minnesota, head of navigation on the Mississippi, was an historic event. "The meeting of the steamboat and the train here in Rock Island is a significant indication of the cooperation that can be achieved between these two groups," proclaimed the President, trying to end the antagonism between railroad and riverboat people. There was little applause, however.

After an hour of speeches, carriages awaited the dignitaries to take them the few blocks to the gangplank to board the large steamboats. The guests ate dinner on board the boats as they crossed the river to the Davenport shoreline. There they enjoyed brief greetings, festivities and later fireworks set off from the abandoned Fort Armstrong.

The Kanes expected to see the procession of boats, go north but looked forward to the fireworks over the river when it became dark. First they would go home, change clothes and have their evening meal.

Colleen was on the lookout for Tom Gannon. She was sure he would not miss this historic happening.

Tom thought he would be able to leave work for the train's arrival because he had asked permission to write about that event. That was the job of a regular reporter, he knew, but he thought he could offer a different point of view, or interview one of the steamboat pilots, the train engineer or the President. His publisher had said that if he got his regular copy laid out, he would allow him to represent the paper as a special reporter. He then gave Tom an official *Rock Island Republican* reporter's card to wear.

At 7 a.m. on the 5th of June, Tom arrived at the newspaper office to do his regular typesetting. He worked fast so that shortly before 4 p.m. he was at the depot beside the engine and first railroad coach, ready for the President to alight. Since Tom wore his newspaper identification card on the front of his hat, the conductor did not shoo him away as he did others. Millard Fillmore was a very stern-looking man with wavy white hair; Tom recognized him right away. Going up to him, he asked, "Mr. President, would you tell me for my newspaper, what are your feelings at this moment about the events of today?"

President Fillmore looked Tom in the eye and replied, "Young man, this is a great moment in history – connecting the Atlantic Coast or, more specifically, the Atlantic Ocean and the great Mississippi River via rail. In a very short time, I'll have the opportunity to view this great country of ours from the wide, wild, wonderful river, on-board one of its majestic steamboats. Needless to say, I am honored and pleased to be a part of this occasion. It will be remembered a hundred years from now. This is the beginning of a 'Grand Excursion.'"

"Thank you, Mr. President," replied Tom, as he finished writing in his notebook what the former head of the United States of America had said. He hoped he'd be able to read his notes when he got back to the newspaper. He had been scribbling quickly and it was hard to concentrate on the words.

It was then Tom spotted the Kane family seated in the special stands. He had not seen Colleen since she visited the newspaper. He thought he would seek them out later, but now he looked for another celebrity to interview. Tom found two more honored guests, who gave comments before the speeches started. When the crowd moved toward the riverboats, Tom worked his way to the family of four.

Colleen had just turned around. "Top of the evening to you all," Tom greeted them.

Everyone was in a jovial mood, but anxious not to miss the gala boat departure. The Kanes at first thought the boat procession would go by their home, but realized that the slough bridge construction there would block the way. They realized that the place to get the best view would be on the former Fort Armstrong island. "Would you like to go with us?" James asked Tom.

"I'm sorry to disappoint you, but the steamboats are only going to cross the river to Davenport now and won't be leaving for the Falls of St. Anthony until late tonight. I would really like to join you, but I'm due back at the newspaper to write up my interviews and finish my work." Then he told them about his special assignment. Colleen could see his excitement. He was so grown up.

Erin blurted out, "I wondered why you had that card on your hat."

When Tom left them, they decided to go to the levee where the boats were lined up, just to see people board and watch the boats cross the wide river to Davenport. By now the streets were free of crowds but not of passing horses and buggies. They had to pick their way carefully when crossing the roads filled with horse excrement. As they passed the general store with barrels of foodstuffs out front, Erin wanted a wooden truck he saw in the window. Maura informed him that they could not afford it and took his hand to encourage him to move on.

The closer the family got to the steamboats, the louder and more boisterous the crowds were. This Rock Island levee was always a busy place, with immigrant and supply boats, large and small, coming and going, but never before had James seen such an assembly of huge steamboats all together with their tall smokestacks alive with smoke. It was thrilling to behold.

Like a fashion parade, each steamship was more gaily decorated than the last. First came the *Golden Era*, with President Fillmore on board. Then there were the *G.W. Sparhawk*, the *Lady Franklin*, the *Galena*, the *Jenny Lind*, the *Black Hawk* and finally the *War Eagle*, which was elegantly decorated with red, white and blue bunting all around. Although the *War Eagle* was last in crossing the river, in the procession upriver it was in the lead because its captain – Daniel Smith Harris, familiar to many people – was experienced at going through the dangerous Rock Island Rapids' fast-moving water and hidden rocks for 14 miles between Davenport and LeClaire.

"Hurrah," shouted Erin, inspired by the sight, making the family all smile.

They watched as the giant steamboats sounded their boat whistles and among loud yelling and laughter peeled off from the Rock Island shore.

James told Erin, "Many a boat has been lost and cargo gone down in this area, so special pilots like Captain Harris was needed to guide the vessels through." He wondered today how safe they would be with such large vessels and possibly inexperienced pilots to the area. James said a little prayer.

At 10 p.m. the steamboats, under a moonlit sky, started upstream with *War Eagle*, under the command of Captain Daniel Smith Harris in the lead. The boats progressed slowly through the dangerous Rock Island Rapids.

But the Kanes did not see them. After the fireworks, they went home and were asleep.

First Railroad Bridge Plan

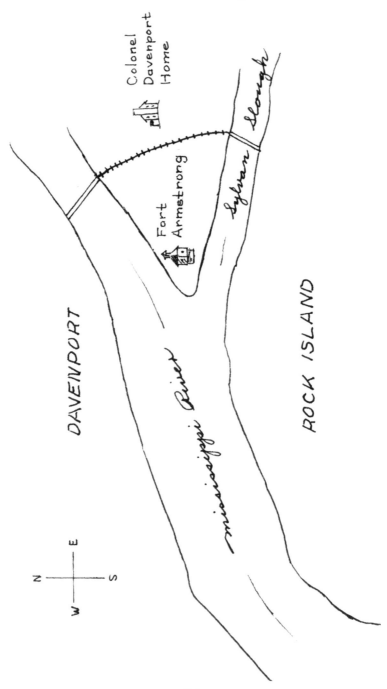

Colonel Davenport Home

Sylvan Slough

Fort Armstrong

DAVENPORT

Mississippi River

ROCK ISLAND

N
W E
S

Chapter 15
FLASHBACK TO 1853
Thursday, 1 September 1853

As James enjoyed the festivities of the Grand Excursion, his mind flashed back to 9 months ago, when his involvement with the railroad began.

It was Thursday the 1st of September 1853. The M&M Railroad, along with the C&RI Railroad, were jointly planning to build the railroad at Rock Island. Today, preparations were beginning on the Davenport end of that span.

After the speeches had been given, Antoine LeClaire threw off his coat to pick up a shovel and dig the first shovelful of dirt for the new bridge to be built between Davenport and Rock Island. The crowd, enlivened by the moment, loved to see LeClaire – the entrepreneur, the interpreter and friend of the Indians, this generous donor of land, their postmaster – do manual labor. The citizens of Davenport shouted and whistled and thoroughly enjoyed the sight. LeClaire, for his part, was huffing and puffing after the first dig, but, for the show, he added a few more shovelsful to the pile.

While the Davenport project continued, the first phase of the Rock Island railroad bridge project began the 28th of September 1853, when John Warner began construction of the piers in Sylvan Slough. This was the first phase of three: building the Sylvan Slough Bridge, laying track on the island and, finally, constructing the main channel bridge.

Warner was aware that this magnificent, but often treacherous, Mississippi was about to be conquered, this river that had limited expansion and defined the country for 77 years. On the other side of the Mississippi, in Iowa, and beyond, fortunes had been made and adventure was awaiting the citizens of the country. But, thus far, this river had been the enslaver. With wood and concrete, Warner had to change that. A bridge would open the gateway to the West...and the people on both the Illinois and Iowa sides of the Mississippi wanted to be the first to create that gateway.

With his crew of mostly Irish and German men, Warner began the Slough Bridge in Rock Island, going east to west, about half a mile from where the first Rock Island Depot would be built, and very close to the Kanes' house. Cofferdams were sunk for the two piers needed in the Sylvan Slough. Warner was following the recommendation that U.S. Engineer Lieutenant Robert E. Lee had made when he surveyed the area in 1837. Lee said that this was the best location to cross the river. The plan was to have the bridge completed in 1855.

Sunday, 25 December 1853

The Kanes had lived in their small house on the river since 1850, when they had arrived from Ireland; therefore, they had seen all of this activity and felt as if they were raising children in the greatest of times.

"Mamma, may I go watch the workers?" was 6-year-old Erin's daily question after school and during vacations, when he had finished his chores. He had found a mound of dirt that was an ideal viewing station. It was high enough above the water that he could get an overview and the men were used to seeing and waving to him. He used to tell them that he was going to build bridges when he grew up.

One time the cofferdam with the men inside started to give way and the men all had to scramble up the ladder to the barge above. No one was hurt, but after that Erin wasn't so sure that was what he wanted to do.

With a sandy bottom, the second pier didn't require the men to dig it out; the cement could be poured inside the drained coffer form directly onto the sand. By December, the piers were showing above the water but winter weather prevented more work from being done until spring.

Christmas at the Kanes' household was a very holy day. It was the birth of Christ and an important day to prepare for. Maura had a small ceramic figure of the Christ Child that she had had since she was a little girl in Ireland. She always treasured it and kept it wrapped in cloth in her dresser drawer. Near November's end in 1853, Maura had James make an eight-inch-long crib out of wood. "The children are old enough to understand and appreciate it now," she told him. The manger was quite crude, just rough wood with no sanding or finish. She put it on the kitchen table and then called a family meeting.

"As we heard Father Alleman say at Mass this morning, today is the beginning of Advent and time to prepare for the coming of the baby

Jesus at Christmas. To help us do that, your father has made this little manger." Erin, only 6 for another week or so, wanted to hold it and see it from the bottom, so Maura let him. Colleen, at 11, could look over his shoulder to see and yet remain more aloof, not seeming so curious but every bit as interested.

Maura continued, "So to prepare and make the bed soft for the Baby, you can add a piece of straw in the manger."

"Oh, let's start right now!" said Erin with his hand on the small yellow mound of straw.

"No, no, Erin, my child, we are all going to earn the straws. For every good deed that you do between now and Christmas Day, you may put a straw in the manger, making the bed soft for the Infant Jesus. That way you are really preparing the way for the Christ Child to come in your heart as well as in this visible crib."

The children were excited. They looked at each other and immediately were trying to think of what they could do to be able to put in a straw.

"Doing your daily chores without complaining can be considered one," interjected James, who was pleased to see the children's eyes sparkling and brains working to come up with ideas. "We do not have to see what you do. It is between you and God, who knows the truth," he added.

The rest of the day was filled with acts of kindness. "You first," said Erin, holding the door for his sister and mother. Erin picked up a towel his mother had dropped. Colleen helped her brother when he had difficulty making his bed. It was a joy for James and Maura to see this comraderie.

At bedtime, Erin asked for the cuddly animal that his mother had made for him. He had trouble sleeping without it anymore. When his father brought it to him, Erin said, "Papa, you can put a straw in the Baby Jesus manger now." James smiled, but did so.

By Christmas Eve the manger was overflowing with straw, reflecting the family's good deeds. When the children got up on Christmas morning, the Infant Jesus lay in His soft bed for the children to see for the first time. Colleen noticed it first. "Oh, Mamma, the Baby Jesus is so sweet. We did really make a soft place for Him!"

"Look, Erin," she called to her brother. "Jesus is in His manger. His feet and arms are reaching up like He wants to be picked up. The only thing He is wearing is a diaper. He must be cold. I'm going to make Him a little blanket."

So Colleen got out her mother's "piece" bag and found a pure white rag, probably an old sheet, tore a small piece off and added an edge of white ribbon. Maura had taught her to sew, and Colleen used the smallest stitches she knew to put it together. "Now Jesus won't be cold," she announced as she laid the soft white blanket on the ceramic figure.

Other than the manger, there were no signs of Christmas. There was no tree, or tinsel, or piles of presents, but everyone had secret gifts hidden away. James had carved for Erin a wooden horse with sturdy legs so he could play with it without breaking them. Maura had knitted colorful mittens for Erin and a red and green plaid wool scarf and matching muff with fringed ends for Colleen.

The children had a hard time thinking of gifts for their parents, but Colleen decided to make a necktie for Papa with Mamma's help. They used one of his ties as a pattern and found a pretty piece of grey silk with a red stripe in it for the material. The amount they needed was small, but the silk was expensive, so they had to pay 10 cents at Buford's General Store. Colleen, under her mother's guidance, cut the material, folded it inside out and with the smallest stitches she knew, stitched the seam. When they went crooked, she took them out and redid them straight. Finishing the side and one end, she turned the tie right-side-out. After slip-stitching the unfinished end, she made two button holes by hand where the tie would overlap onto his shirt. She was proud of her work, though she knew her buttonholes were not perfect.

To think of something to do secretly for Mamma was harder since she was there at home all the time. The children thought and thought of a gift but finally decided to ask Papa.

"We can't think of anything to get or make for Mamma for Christmas, Papa. Can you help us?" asked Colleen when Papa was outside cleaning the cistern for winter.

"I have been thinking of what to get her, too, Colleen. A warm coat or new cape is what I would like to have made for her, but I don't have enough money. I have been saving a little out of each paycheck toward it but have less than four weeks to go."

"Maybe we can help you, Papa," exclaimed Colleen.

"I have 20 cents from my birthday that will help," offered Erin.

"And I found 10 cents on the boardwalk in town," said Colleen. "My birthday isn't until January, but maybe I could work to earn some money. Mr. McGregor offered to pay someone to grade math papers. I didn't volunteer yet but was going to ask you and Mamma if I could." Colleen looked anxiously at her father.

"Even with help from both of you, I am afraid we can't make it. But I saw a hand mirror in a glass case at the store last time I was in town. That was much less expensive. Maybe we can get her that. As to your working, Colleen, your mother will need to agree to that. We do not want anything to interfere with your education. When were you thinking you would do it?"

"Oh, Papa, I could stay in at recess or after school maybe. It wouldn't take too long each day. Will you talk to Mamma about it?"

Colleen's job was eventually approved by Maura as long as it didn't affect her own school work. By Christmas Eve, at 5 cents for each set of papers, Colleen had earned 90 cents, and with her found money, she could contribute $1.00 to the mirror. James picked out the gift so that the children could still be surprised when the package was opened.

Maura, herself, was making a dress shirt for James and worked on it during the day when the family was gone. Mr. Buford had given her a bargain on white cotton broadcloth on a bolt from the previous season. It was certainly a labor of love, all handmade with flat-fell seams, beautifully finished buttonholes and Mississippi River mussel-shell buttons. Even she was pleased with the results.

Before gifts were opened, however, they attended Mass at St. James. The church was packed for the one Mass of the day. Catholics from farms all over the region came at Christmas and saw the simple altar banked with flowers. A Christmas creche, which one of the parishioners had carved, was set up with the three important figures only. That man agreed that next year he would make some animal figures to add to the scene.

Erin whispered to Colleen, "The Baby Jesus carved in wood is not nearly as pretty as the one in our crib at home." Colleen agreed, but thought the almost-life-size, painted figures were beautiful as well.

Everyone was very jovial, greeting even those they did not know with a "Blessed Christmas!" There had been no snow as yet this winter, but as they came out of church it had already started to snow and the Kanes enjoyed their walk home in the white flakes. It was good for packing and Erin, Colleen and even James got into making and throwing some at hitching posts and they even had a friendly snowball fight. Maura stayed out of the way. "Glory be, when the lot of you are finished, I'll have a good hot cup of tea to warm you up," Maura said as she entered their house.

The threesome stayed outside playing in the snow, having a friendly fight with Erin and Colleen against their father, until, wet and cold, they came in laughing. "We won! We won!" the children were shouting. "I must admit, this Irishman was beat by his own children. What do you think of that, Maura?" exclaimed James, humbly and with a wink.

"It warms the cockles of my heart to hear the fun you were having. Now, let's get those wet things off and you can warm up by the fire. I have fresh tea and scones for us all, and then we have some presents to open."

Christmas gifts had been forgotten for a while with the arrival of the long-awaited snow. But now Colleen and Erin, as well as James and Maura, were excited. It was not for what they would be getting, but for how the gifts they had for others would be received.

As the youngest, Erin was allowed to go first. Opening his newspaper-wrapped carved horse first, he immediately chanted "Giddy up, giddy up" and "Whoa" as he playfully rode the miniature horse over the table and down on the wet, snow-tracked floor.

Colleen was next. As she was unwrapping her beautiful matching scarf and muff, a loud noise outside interrupted their festivities. They could not imagine what it could be on Christmas Day and in the snow. So James went to investigate. Unbarring and opening the door, James was shocked to see two Indians, one old and one a young brave, standing there in their native costume covered in snow. James clutched the door tightly, but something about their posture told him these two were not hostile. In fact, the older man seemed familiar.

"Could you be Loud Thunder?" James wondered aloud.

Several weeks before, while James and his men were laying track on the other side of Moline, a small group of Indians appeared at a distance on horseback. They were curious about what the workmen were doing and watched them for a while. The workmen were nervous, not knowing if they were friendly or not. James' men had no weapons except heir shovels. James tried to reassure his crew that the Indians were merely interested in what they were doing. The next day, however, when they came back, one of the men had brought a gun from home, unbeknownst to James and against the rules James had set.

On the second day, the Indians had come closer. James even went up to them to speak to the head of the party. It was "Loud Thunder," son of Black Hawk, who had died 15 years before. James welcomed them and tried to explain what the men were doing. "Track for 'big' engine," and he demonstrated the size "big" with his arms up and out to show the enormity of the locomotive . . . "bigger than the buffalo" which he showed with his hands bent above his head for horns, and rubbing first one foot in the dirt and then the other, like an animal getting ready to charge.

As James was making sounds like the train whistle "Woo woo," the Indians started to laugh at his antics and noises. They had no idea what a train was and couldn't picture anything bigger than a buffalo that could move. But at least all was friendly.

For the next few days, the visits continued but only for short periods of time. Then the Indians left, not to return. James found out about the gun and reprimanded the worker. "If any incident had happened with the gun, you would have been out of a job," he told him. "Take it home and don't bring it back!"

James invited the Indians at his door to come in and introduced his family to them. He had not told Maura or the children about the Indian visits because he didn't want to scare them. "Loud Thunder and a party of Indians visited the track site a few weeks ago," was all he said now.

Loud Thunder said something in his native language as a greeting James was sure, then they were silent. Maura felt very ill at ease with her quiet company, but she knew that food is something that all people understand. So she made more tea and served it. The duck that James had hunted for their Christmas meal was cooking on a spit in the fireplace. The smell was starting to permeate the single-room house and even caused Maura to wonder if that was what had brought the Indians to their door. Could they have smelled it outside? Potatoes and corn were to round out the meal. She had made an apple pie yesterday, for which she was glad now.

James asked if the two would like to stay for dinner and demonstrated eating with a spoon going to his mouth and pointing to them and to his own family. Loud Thunder nodded in agreement.

All the while, Colleen and Erin were in a state of disbelief. Their parents' confidence and lack of fear erased the children's fear almost right away. Two members of the Sauk-Fox tribe were visiting in their house. It was unbelievable! Neither child could take their eyes off their guests' clothing. Both men had on long buckskin jackets fringed at the bottom. The elder man had short sleeves with the ends cut to long points about four inches deep, under which was a long-sleeved garment needed in this weather. Darker deerskin pants, leather moccasins and a three-inch-wide scarf-like piece heavily beaded with star motifs hung to within six inches of the bottom of his jacket and completed his attire. It was his headgear that was most striking. It was a full-feathered, front-beaded headpiece, mostly white, with cords of beads and his own graying braids of hair that hung over his shoulder.

The young brave, about 16 years of age, had fitted and fringed chaps or pants. His buckskin top was deeply fringed and belted in at the waistline. The sleeves were long and simple and his moccasins beautifully beaded. His shiny long black hair was braided and a single white feather stood up in back, held in place by a decorated band of animal hide.

During the meal, the Indians didn't speak, but Erin had so many things he wanted to know. What were they doing out in the snow today? Where do they live? How did they find our house? Do they know it is Christmas?

James wanted to know many of the same things, but at the table was not the time to act out his questions. So the meal was quite silent. Their guests followed what the family did. They passed their plates back to James for more duck when they finished the first helping. But the other dishes had little left for seconds. They especially enjoyed Maura's homemade bread and had numerous pieces.

After the meal, the family wanted to continue opening their Christmas gifts but had no presents for their guests until Maura thought of the potato candy that she had made as a secret treat. So she went behind Colleen's screen and made up two packages, one of green color and one of pink, tinted with berries and mint. Using cord and a printed cloth from her piece bag, she wrapped them.

While she was doing this, James was acting out some of his questions. Loud Thunder understood at least one. He indicated that he was showing his grandson the land that was his people's former garden. It may have been James' imagination, but he believed that he saw a tear in this elderly Indian's eyes when he recalled the past.

The two visitors were not sure what they were to do with the gifts when they were handed them. Erin spoke up and said, "You open it," and along with his words he exaggeratedly demonstrated pulling the bow of the cord. The two guests followed his gestures, making the family laugh at the exaggerated motion they used to untie the sisal cord. Then Erin showed them the candy was to be eaten, and he made circles over his own stomach, saying "Ummmm." The guests did the same and again everyone laughed.

Colleen finished opening the beautifully woven scarf and muff. She put the scarf around her neck and then showed how the quilted-and-lined muff warmed her hands. Colleen was very happy with her present.

James was next and truly appreciated the shirt that Maura had made and the tie from Colleen. He said, "My helpmate and little lass know how to make me happy. Thank you both."

Lastly, Maura opened her store-wrapped gift. "What could it be?"

When she saw the mirror, she was delighted. "Faith and begorrah, it is a hand-mirror." Immediately she looked at her image and secured the strand of hair that had fallen around her face.

Their guests by now were aware of it being a special gift-giving time, but they had come unprepared. Loud Thunder, the elder of the two, reached up to pull two colored feathers from his headdress. Then he took several strands of beads from his neck. He presented the feathers to James and Erin with somber formality, and the beads to Maura and Colleen, who thanked them mostly with their smiles, since words were not understood.

Then, without commotion, the two Indians left the house and rode away on their horses.

It had been an unusual and blessed Christmas for the Kanes.

Chapter 16
SLOUGH BRIDGE
Friday 23 June 1854

It was in late June 1854, after the Grand Excursion, that the Slough Bridge was nearing completion. The scaffolding came down, revealing a flat-topped bridge with a Howe truss design. Arches of wood were added on each side of the bridge for support. "The arches will reinforce the bridge so that it should last for years," reported Mr. Warner to James one day when James came to see the progress. Laying supports for the track on the deck was the last work that needed to be done.

At the supper table the family heard the latest developments from Erin. "Mr. Warner came up onto my hill today to see what I see and gave me an apple."

However, the most wonderful day was when Erin announced, "The men cleaned up all their tools today and left waving goodbye. Mamma, can we all go on the new bridge, now?"

Maura looked at James, who nodded his approval. "Blessed be the saints, but I think we can do that on Sunday after Mass."

Erin couldn't wait for Father Alleman to finish celebrating Mass the following Sunday. All he could think of was their family trip across 'his' bridge today. James was equally interested because he would be laying track on it as soon as approval was given. The Kanes spoke to the Gannon family a few minutes. Erin wanted Sean to come with him on their tour of the bridge, and Colleen invited Tom. It was agreeable with the children and parents alike, as long as Tom would watch over his younger brother.

The now enlarged Kane family walked toward the river two by two on the boardwalk as far as it existed and then continued on bare ground. James and Maura led the way, avoiding horse and buggies out for a Sunday morning ride. Next were Erin and Sean, excited and jumping around, and finally, Colleen and Tom, making sure their siblings stayed in tow. They went Rock River Street to Davenport Street and down it, across the train tracks to the Kanes' house. It was a beautiful June morning, but still Maura wanted to get her shawl because of the cool air she knew she would feel from the river.

Then James took Maura's hand and led the way over the rough ground, past construction debris, up to the bridge entrance. Not surprising to James, but to the rest, was a barricade of dirt mounded to prevent such expeditions. The children enjoyed climbing the packed mud, only to discover that there was no finished deck on which to walk. There were only heavy planks laid end to end across the wooden horizontal struts. James would be laying the heavy metal narrow gauge railroad track down the middle, 4 feet 8 inches apart.

Maura wasn't sure she wanted to do this. But the wind was nil, the river smooth and glittery in the sunshine, so single file, holding hands, they crossed the first span and continued across the second. It was not the time to look down at the moving water, but Colleen did. She let out a sharp squeal, which stopped the whole line. Tom gently encouraged her not to look down again, but to stay focused on her mother. She was doing very well up ahead of Erin, whose hand was perspiring greatly.

The procession continued the rest of the way without incident. After the third bridge span there was a sandbar and the island edge. They all got off in relief. They had made it across the Sylvan Slough – the first civilians to cross the bridge. Erin was jumping on the hard sand and telling his friend, Sean, how he had watched all of this being built. Maura appreciated much more now what her husband would be struggling with daily.

They had accomplished what they had set out to do, but didn't want to go right back. So James led the way to Fort Armstrong. It had been abandoned by the soldiers at this time because the Sauk and Fox had been driven off and were no longer a threat. However the fort buildings remained. James told the others the history.

"Fort Armstrong was built in 1815 after the Indians attacked Lieutenant Campbell, not too far up the river, during the War of 1812," James began. "This used to be the recreation area for the Indians – in fact, all of Rock Island, Moline and even across the river was a part of their land. When the Indians left, white settlers moved into their teepees as tentative homes until they could build their own. There are still people living on the island. Colonel George Davenport's family has a large house fairly close. The Colonel, himself, was murdered in his home on the 4th of July nine years ago."

"Murdered?" asked Erin and Sean together. This was turning out to be more than a bridge adventure for the boys.

"Yes, Colonel Davenport was home alone on the 4th of July 1845, because his family was in town for an Independence Day celebration. He heard a noise in a back room and went to investigate. He found the bandits and before he could draw his pistol, they shot him in the thigh. They dragged him upstairs and forced him to open his safe, but found only $600. When he refused to tell them where more money was, they left with a gold watch, a double-barrel gun and other small things. Colonel Davenport died later from the loss of blood. But he lived long enough to name the men who had robbed him."

"Did they find the men?" asked Sean.

"Thanks be to God they did. The citizens were horrified and sent out search parties. Two months later they found the leaders, Robert Birch and John Long, one of whom they believe fired the gun. They were hanged in October of the same year. They say 5,000 people attended. The others were found, two in Galena and one in Nauvoo, five men all together."

The boys were glad justice reigned. "It's a good story, but sad," said Erin. Maura was now eager to get back to the safety of their home. On the way back, James told them that the track for the railroad would curve across the island to the place where the main bridge crossing would be. "There will be new contractors for the main channel bridge and experienced men from New England to build the main channel piers. Everything is ready," James told them. Maura noticed the gleam in her husband's eyes. He loved being part of this "making of history."

Chapter 17
INDEPENDENCE
Tuesday, 4 July 1854

It was the 4th of July and the Kanes planned a picnic with the Gannons.

"Mamma, what are we taking to the picnic to eat? And where are we going?" asked Colleen. She was thinking about Tom and wanted the day to be perfect.

"Glory be, child, but we're having what you and Erin like in the summer, potato salad. Then I'm making navy beans which your father likes so much. The beans have been soaking overnight and I started them cooking early with salt pork and molasses. They should be done about noon. You can help peel the potatoes, Colleen. The Gannons are bringing baked chicken. They raise chickens on their place, so Mrs. Gannon offered. I'm glad our potato crop was good last year because we have plenty. This year's crop seems to be doing fine because we are watering it regularly from the river. Thank goodness for the river."

"As to where we are going...Washington Square. It is so handy. Without a wagon it would be hard for us to get to any other park. The Gannons have farther to go, but they won't be walking."

"Mamma, Mr. McGregor always tells us how important this day is to our country. He calls it 'Independence Day' and sometimes tells stories of men who fought in the Revolutionary War. He knew people in Boston, when he was growing up, who fought in the war. But he said that he has heard of a man who lives in DeWitt, Iowa, named John Lepper, who enlisted in the patriot army of 1776 for three terms, a big decision for him since he was British. And a daughter of Betsy Ross, who made our country's first flag, lives in Fort Madison, Iowa.

"A man named Daniel Dow lives here in Iowa. During the Revolution, when he was only seven years old, he carried important messages from one American military leader to another. When Mr. McGregor told us that story, the boys in the class, including Erin, were all wishing we were at war so they could be a part of it.

Maura frowned. "No one should wish for a war," she said firmly.

Colleen continued. "It was just play, Mamma." At recess that was what they pretended – they were Paul Revere riding to warn the colonists, George Washington crossing the Delaware, patriots fighting at Bunker Hill, but mostly they wanted to be Daniel Dow carrying messages. No one wanted to be the Red Coats. We girls stood around and cheered for the Americans. Mr. McGregor always makes us feel so proud to be citizens of the United States."

"As well you should be!" responded Maura. "This is the country we have adopted and love dearly. I am so glad that Mr. McGregor is so patriotic. Do you know exactly what we celebrate this day?"

At this moment Erin appeared in his nightclothes. "I know what happened. The Declaration of Independence was adopted on this day, the 4th of July, in 1776."

"But Mamma asked me, Erin, not you," Colleen pouted. "I've been telling her all about what we've learned from Mr. McGregor. That's not fair that you answer."

"That is all right, Colleen, I know you know. It is good to find out that your brother is paying attention." Colleen still glared at her brother.

"It is time that you feed Miracle, Erin," said Maura. "Your father has gone to check on some noise he heard on the Slough Bridge. It is blocked, but sometimes children try to get on it and dive into the water. The water is low with our drought, and we don't want anyone getting hurt." Maura seemed a little concerned that James was not back yet.

Shortly after Erin took feed and water to the chicken, James came home through the gate and across the back yard where Miracle and Erin were running around chasing each other. First the chicken would follow Erin, who started slow and got faster and faster, then Erin turned and ran after Miracle. It was humorous to watch, and James was all smiles when he came inside.

Maura asked James what had kept him so long.

"Boys from up on Orleans Street climbed over the mound of dirt barracking the bridge. They were fooling around on the bridge itself – running on the planks, skimming rocks out into the water – and were just talking about going skinny dipping when I arrived. I pointed out that they were breaking the law by being on the bridge at all and that the water was low and very dangerous to dive into. They didn't like it that I made them leave. I stayed to be sure that they didn't come back."

At about 11:30, Maura and Colleen had packed everything for the outing. Maura carried the potato salad in a large squash shell covered with a lid. James managed the bean pot, which had an outer container to protect him from the heat. Colleen had the tablecloth with four plates and the silverware tied into it and Erin had a printed calico cloth holding some tin cups ready for water or the lemonade that the Gannons were bringing.

The last thing that James told Erin was to be sure to secure the gate so that Miracle would not get out. Erin ran to do it, saying goodbye to the chicken and waving at him.

When the family arrived at the park, they were happy to find the Gannons were already there and had located a place for the picnic. It was on a low rise in the ground, under the shade of a giant oak tree. It faced the river, so that they could catch a view of the water between buildings. Barbara Gannon greeted Maura with open arms and the "Glory be's" flowed. The two ladies immediately started spreading the tablecloths and organizing the food, knowing everyone was hungry.

James and Bill Gannon shook hands and talked shop. The long awaited main-channel bridge work was starting, and they were happy about that.

Erin and Sean were quickly involved in a game of "tag."

Sean's younger brothers – John, age 4, and Patrick, age 5 – wanted to play, too, so the older boys slowed down and allowed themselves to be easily caught. Sometimes Sean made believe he was just too tired to run anymore, so he would be tagged. All were really having a great time.

Tom and Colleen enjoyed watching the foursome. But Tom's responsibility was looking after Frankie, who was two years old and a challenge. Colleen helped prevent the toddler from major falls on the rough ground. She took away a piece of glass he found buried in the grass and wiped away a tear when a gnarled tree root caused him to fall and skin a knee.

The ladies only had to say once that it was time to eat and everyone formed a line. Maura dished up the beans and potato salad while Barbara did the honors with the chicken and pickled watermelon rind she had brought. Bill Gannon poured the lemonade. James led everyone in thanksgiving for the food they were about to eat. Then everyone sat on the ground and ate.

The park was quickly filling up with many others, most of whom the Kanes knew at least by sight.

"Did everyone wake up at sunrise this morning with the ringing of the church bells?" asked Tom as he sat on the ground with his overloaded plate of food.

"It made chills go up and down my spine!" said Maura. "I thought about how free we are here in this country today. We have so much to be grateful for."

"I didn't hear it," said Erin.

"You didn't hear it, Erin? It woke me up and I put my pillow over my head," complained Sean.

"Yes, I read in the newspaper that it was planned, but I forgot about it. The loud bells from the different churches ringing woke me up. Then I realized what day it was, smiled and went back to sleep," reported Bill Gannon.

"You know the town is planning a parade this afternoon. I think we can go see it when we are done eating. It starts at one p.m. at Rock Street and down Washington Street to the river, back up and over to Courthouse Square. The children would enjoy it, I think," said James.

"Yay, yay," shouted Erin, Sean and the little boys all in unison while nodding and looking at each other with smiles of anticipation.

After this announcement, the young boys had trouble eating much more. They did, however, have a piece of Mrs. Gannon's chocolate cake. . . or at least the frosting.

When it came time to clean up, not much was left over. All their utensils and plates were tied up in the Kanes' cloth and put in the Gannon wagon with the bean pot and the Gannon picnic equipment. The horse and flatbed wagon were waiting at the road edge. The plan was that Tom with Colleen would drive the children around the Square and over Orleans Street to watch. This way the children had a place to sit. The adults stood at the wagon's end.

The parade consisted of fifteen different groups or floats. In the beginning a band played "The Star-Spangled Banner" to get everyone into the mood. The mayor and city council were on a decorated horse-drawn wagon. The crowd went wild to see the next cart, which had three soldiers of the American Revolution. All were in their 90's. People clapped and yelled at the sight. Following them, the orator who was going to do the reading of the Declaration of Independence at the courthouse rode horseback and caused a stir among the crowd. The clergy came next, walking and waving. Father Alleman was one of them.

"Hi, Father!" yelled Sean and Erin and the Gannon young ones. Even Frankie waved. They were excited and pleased to see someone that they knew in the parade.

Men from the judicial court in their robes and other officers of the court rode the next float. From then on the parade marchers were visitors from other countries or cities or the parade committee. Then members of the press passed by, and it was time for Tom to yell and wave to those he knew. Lastly, another band consisting of two snare drums, a bass drum and a fife played "Yankee Doodle" and left people's hearts pounding in patriotic emotion.

Everyone was tired by this time and ready to go home. So the adults piled aboard the wagon and Tom drove to the Kane home.

When the horse pulled up to the back of the house, Erin was the first one to notice that the gate was open. Rather than waiting to be helped down – the wagon bed was about five feet above the ground – Erin jumped down and ran into the yard. What he saw made him scream. "Miracle, oh, Miracle, what happened to you?"

The chicken lay on the ground in a pool of blood. Her neck was broken and chest punctured by some animal's teeth. Feathers were scattered on the ground.

The rest of the family, as well as the Gannons, came into the yard, but turned around to keep the little ones from seeing what had happened. It was difficult for everyone. Colleen went over to Erin and tried to hug his shoulders, but he shrugged her off. He then got down on the ground and cuddled the chicken. No one said anything.

Nothing anyone could say would help.

"Erin, are you sure you locked the gate?" asked James.

"I'm sure of it, Papa!" Erin replied, with tears running down his face.

Puzzled and sad, the rest of the family took the picnic things into the house and left Erin to grieve outside.

"What comes to my mind are the boys that wanted to go swimming and I prevented them this morning," said James. "Do you think they could have watched when I came home and purposely opened the gate to get back at me? There are wild dogs around all the time, just ready for such an opportunity. I feel so bad! Erin was so attached to the chicken and to have it happen on this day of all days."

"Well, maybe, if it had to happen, this is not such a bad day," said Maura. "I think it is time we bury the poor thing and talk to Erin about this."

"James, would you get the shovel and see what Erin wants to do, where he wants to bury her? It will have to be deep so other predators don't dig it up."

Erin wanted to bury Miracle in the yard, in the corner where the chicken always slept. With his father's help, he dug a grave and made a sign, 'Miracle Sleeps Here.'

By this time night had fallen and everyone came inside.

"You know, Erin, this is 'Independence Day' for us all, and mostly for Miracle. He has gotten his 'Independence' today. He is no longer confined to the yard, to the little feed you gave him, or to eating when you say. He is in 'Chicken Heaven' where he can roam wherever he wants and eat anything he wants, when he wants. He is free!" said Maura. As if to punctuate what she said, a cannon blast from the former Fort Armstrong resounded throughout the house and area and ended the day's celebrations. Erin took it as a salute to Miracle and went to bed thinking he was grateful to have had his chicken friend for a short while.

Chapter 18
THE INJUNCTION
Wednesday, 5 July 1854

Once the holiday was over, the Chicago and Rock Island Railroad was pressing to get track laid on the new Slough Bridge and across the island. Henry Farnam, President and Chief Engineer, saw to it that James Kane was hired for the job. James was allowed to pick his own crew and work commenced. Erin again took his spot on his private mountain to view the progress, which helped him forget his sadness at Miracle's death.

Sean Gannon came again one day to watch the men working. The two boys were getting to be very good friends. "You are lucky to live so close to all that is going on, Erin," said Sean. "I'm glad we are friends and that you invite me over."

The new track, once laid, was used immediately by the coal-burning locomotive and flatbed cars to bring the heavy supplies across the Slough Bridge to the island and then across the land. Hand-powered carts brought smaller supplies and James, himself, to and from the location.

As the track crossed the island slightly west of Colonel Davenport's beautiful home high on a knoll, James could see the town of Davenport laid out before him across the river. It was an active place, with lumber mills close to the river. Antoine LeClaire owned a small house, barely visible near the foot of the hill, but was beginning construction of his brick Italianate mansion rising at the top of the hill. Giant log rafts arrived often, some 1000 feet long, and were stored in riverside pens until the lumberyards could cut them into boards. Steamboats daily brought immigrants to both river towns, Rock Island and Davenport.

James realized that once the main channel bridge was built, there would even be more growth in Davenport with the movement of people heading west.

For the first time, James thought, "I would like to live across the river."

James and one of his men work the hand cart

Thursday, 20 July 1854

Before the island track was finished and the first piers were begun in the main channel, young Tom Gannon showed James a newspaper article dated 20 July 1854, saying that Jefferson Davis, Secretary of War under President Franklin Pierce, had ordered a federal injunction. It said, "The railroad is trespassing on government property. Work on the bridge between Rock Island and Davenport shall cease. The work force shall disband," Tom read.

Immediately James told Tom, "But this is just a concocted method of stopping the bridge from being built. The government abandoned Fort Armstrong in 1836 when it was thought that the Indians were no longer a threat to the citizens. The soldiers left, leaving the island to 'squatters.' It is no longer a military base. Besides, the railroad has gotten a 'right of way' across the island from the state and the federal government. How can Jefferson Davis say that?"

The legal action slowed the bridge work while the railroad awaited the court's decision. But it didn't stop progress. James continued the work on the track across the island. He was afraid every day that a marshal might come to stop him and his men and order them off the island, but it never happened.

The railroad had already hired Louis and Thomas Saulbaugh, brothers from New England, as James had told his family earlier, to build the piers in the main channel. The injunction held them off until late summer of 1855; when the railroad administrators felt confident that the courts would rule in their favor, they allowed work to begin again. The bridge was to be built at the foot of the Rock Island Rapids with a current fast enough to drive a millwheel. It took the expertise of men who had done this type of work before under difficult conditions to be successful.

As work progressed and piers started to grow out of the water, riverboat pilots continued to guide boats around the twisted channel of rocks, but now they had to avoid the piers as well. Even as they were being built, accidents happened and boats hit the newly installed piers, infuriating the riverboat community. The Kanes only heard about such accidents from James because they had the island between them and the main channel and were not able to see the work being done. "A steamboat coming from Minnesota hit one of the piers today," James said at the dinner table one fall evening. The boat was hardly damaged but the pier work was set back again for repairs. "I sometimes wonder if these accidents are accidents at all. These are expert pilots taking the boats through the rapids and they can see the piers standing at least 15 feet above water."

"I miss being able to see the men at work," chimed in Erin. "It was fun watching from my little mountain as they built the Slough Bridge. Even my hill of dirt is gone now. They took it all away," Erin related with sadness.

"Erin, you know that 'mountain,' as you called it, was really dirt from digging the abutment and piers, and was needed to build the approaches when the bridge was done," James explained as gently as possible. He knew how attached Erin had become to the location.

Chapter 19
GROWTH
Sunday, 31 December 1854

The year 1854 had seen tremendous growth, especially in Davenport. Three hundred new buildings were constructed and, unlike in hard times, there were no vacant buildings or business rooms. James started to watch for a house he might like and could afford in Davenport. He heard about an Octagon House, only six blocks up from the river, the form of which was supposed to be conducive to good health. Its design had been inspired by a traveling phrenologist, Orson Fowler, author of the book *Home For All*. The house was not for sale, having just been built by a leading Davenport merchant, H. H. Smith, but James told Maura about it. They joked that if eight sides is good for one's health, a round house would be even better. However, building anything was financially out of the question for the Kanes.

Packet boats carrying passengers, freight and mail left New Orleans weekly for the Davenport/Rock Island area, while boats came daily from St. Louis to Davenport and went on up to LeClaire. The people-growth was phenomenal in Davenport and its physical appearance also changed with the addition of gaslights on the streets. One person was assigned to light the lamps at dusk, making streets safer and providing a romantic subject for music writers.

In addition to railroad growth, stagecoach lines were now criss-crossing the whole state of Iowa, having already done so in Illinois and further east. The horse-and-carriage was still the normal means of long-distance transportation in 1854. The Mississippi River had been the barrier to growth until now. But once the bridge was built, overcoming that wide water obstruction, James knew that trains would quickly take over.

"Weather is one thing that man cannot change," stated James one day to Erin when discussing the area's growth. It was tornado season, and the sky looked threatening. From their location on the river's edge, the Kanes had a 180-degree view of the heavens. First there was that eerie yellow glow in the sky, then it got darker and darker and very windy. "We had better take shelter. It looks bad." So the family went down into the small fruit cellar below their house. Being below ground was the safest place during tornadoes, James knew.

"If Miracle were here, she would be squawking and upset," said Erin. James responded, "Yes, chickens or animals of any kind sense the weather change and are afraid." The family then hurried down into the root cellar.

When the threat was over and the sky had cleared and the winds had died down, they found tree branches scattered everywhere, but nothing worse. They were very grateful, and it was at that point that James recalled having heard a story about how the area was protected from natural disasters.

"It was nineteen years ago, back in 1835, even before St. Anthony's Church was built, that Father Charles Van Quickenborne stood on the ground on the other side of Antoine LeClaire's estate and raised a crucifix, blessing the area against anything disastrous that comes from nature – fire, tornado, earthquake." James continued, "I'm told at one time a fire in East Davenport threatened to destroy the downtown, coming from the Eastside lumberyards. But it miraculously stopped just short of where Father Quickenborne blessed the land. I expect someday an altar will be built there to honor the power of that blessing."

"Can we go see it, Papa?" asked Erin with great hope.

"Now there is not much to see but weedy ground and maybe a marker. When we find a place to live in Davenport, maybe we can go sometime," responded James.

Once James was done laying the track across the island for the C&RI Railroad – where he had been paid in money, not calico! – he was back across the river, working for the M&M Railroad, setting the track to Iowa City. Work had ceased when James had left, giving the M&M Railroad administrators time to try to raise money to pay the workers. They were not too successful, however, so calico continued to be the payment.

As the distance from home became greater, James and his men stayed weekdays in the area in which they were working, coming home on weekends only. The deadline for the track to be completed was the 31st of December, 1855, at midnight. However, bad weather slowed down the work and it looked like the goal would not be reached on time. But the Iowa City townspeople helped. The engine froze up and "pinch bars" coaxed the locomotive along and temporary rails were laid to close the 200-yard gap. The "dead" locomotive was prodded along and made the deadline to the station and end of the track amid church bells and

New Year celebrations. However, the locomotive engineer collapsed by his engine and had to be carried to the depot. "His name was Charles Stickles," said James, as he related this to his family. Henry Farnam was there to personally supervise the arrival.

The 3rd of January, 1856, with a temperature of 18 degrees below zero, a special train from Davenport came over the makeshift track. Cannon boomed, the train stopped and people marched to the "Old Capitol" as three bands played to celebrate the arrival of both the train and the New Year.

Chapter 20
CROSSING
July 1855 – March 1856

Jefferson Davis, Secretary of War, had claimed that the island off of Rock Island was for military use only, that it was not public domain, and the court mandated that construction cease. If that position were upheld, the railroad could not cross it and the bridgework would be forced to stop forever. However, in July 1855, Associate Justice John McLean ruled that the railroad did indeed have a right to cross the island on land which the government owned. His ruling stated that "railroads have become highways in something of the same sense as rivers; neither can suffer to be a permanent obstruction to the other, but each must yield something to the other: according to the demands of public convenience and necessities of commerce."

Tom proudly showed the article to James and said, "So now the bridge can be finished. I am so happy for our towns, the country and for you, James. It has been hard being in and out of work these last few years, I'm sure. Have you thought about getting into the newspaper business? I mean, once the bridge work is finished? Or maybe while you're waiting for work. It is steady work, and I think the editor would be glad to have you. He is as proud as anybody about the bridge and your part in it, which he mentioned having heard about."

Maura and James had discussed James's future and had come to the conclusion that even if the bridge would be finished, which they were confident that it would, that the bridge would be the last major track to be laid in the area. Then what would he do? He was intrigued by the big presses at the newspaper and thought that would be interesting and steady work, so he had applied as an apprentice printer.

Tom Gannon liked his work at the *Davenport Gazette*, after having been at the *Rock Island Republican* for several years. His publisher, who recently returned from Minnesota, told Tom, "Minneapolis has finished a bridge span across the narrower part of the Mississippi River up there. It is a wagon bridge – not for heavy trains, but rather a wooden suspension type. Carriages, horse-drawn wagons, people and animals of all sorts cross it for a fee. It, therefore, officially is the first bridge across the Mississippi River. Had we not been delayed with this crazy injunction, we would have had the first bridge."

"Ours will be the first railroad bridge, though," countered Tom.

When the injunction was lifted in July, construction on the piers for the main channel bridge proceeded without fear of the courts stopping them. However, building piers was not an easy task at the foot of the rapids with a current that could drive a mill wheel. Despite accidents with boats and have to constantly fight the current, by December the piers were all in place, rising well above high-water level.

But now thick ice had covered the river. How could bridgework continue? Mr. Brayton, resident engineer, had the answer. He would use the ice to his advantage.

He bought the best pair of horses he could find to help build the falsework scaffolding for the superstructure.

Next he needed an expert with horses. Charles Williams, the stonecutter for the construction, said his brother-in-law, Gustavius Allbee, was just such a person. Therefore, G. Allbee moved here from Vermont with his wife and four children and was put up in a shanty on Government Island.

It was late December 1855 when Mr. Allbee took control of the team on the ice. It was a winter where the ice remained thick for six weeks, allowing work to progress safely. Allbee and his excellent horses raised beams 12 inches square and 32 feet long with precision. Men at either end would attach block and tackle with yards of rope. Huge beams could be uprighted into place or moved across the top of others to build the falsework and then the bridge itself all on the ice.

Allbee loved the horses and called them by name, Prince and Maler. "Whoa, boys. Come just a trifle. Back, boys. Whoa, hold it." Mr. Allbee knew exactly how to control them. The bridge took shape during the winter months, a feat most people would have thought was not possible.

The Allbee family and the Kanes met one Sunday in early March when both had come to the Government Island riverbank to see the construction closer. The long hard winter was about to give way. Soon the weather would be getting warmer and the ice would no longer support the heavy horses. In fact, this day was sunny and turning out to be a little above freezing. Mr. Allbee checked the ice at the bank and realized it would be dangerous to take the horses out on it any longer.

James Kane went down to the river's embankment and introduced himself. He told Mr. Allbee that he had heard about his excellent work with the teams from some railroad officials. James told him that he was waiting until the bridge was complete so he could lay the track. The men became friends immediately and walked up to where their families were watching from a little distance. Introductions were made all around, but Erin had already made friends with Elbert Allbee, a six-year-old.

Gus, as Mr. Allbee asked to be called, explained that the giant swingspan was all that was left to be built. They all walked out on the temporary wooden deck to near the middle of the river. Workmen had already strung two great rope cables three feet apart, from the second Illinois span, across the middle chasm, to the next span on the Iowa side. Short pieces of plank were secured across them and longer boards placed lengthwise on top, forming a rope suspension bridge for the crew to cross. "The only support is a rope handrail, as you can see, which was completed last night," said Gus.

But Mr. Allbee had something else in mind. He had overheard some of the men talking yesterday about bringing their wives on Monday and taking them across the rope span. He was here now and so was his wife. Why not have her be the first woman to cross the Mississippi River on a railroad bridge. Knowing that it would be a scary thing for her, he asked if she would like to cross on the ropes with him.

Eliza Malvina Allbee was only 28 years old, petite and agile. She had left a comfortable home in Vermont to follow her husband here to little more than wilderness. She said, "What was there so frightening about a moving bridge?" She was willing and almost immediately she grasped the hand rope and steadfastly trudged across the unsteady bridge.

Gus followed with a firm hand on his six-year-old son, Elbert, who looked down at the cold, now-broken moving ice but felt safe with his father's big hand over his. They swung first one way then the other but managed to get across. The rest of the bridge was like the first, no great challenge but still not too safe with loose boards spaced out as a walk. They returned to the Kanes the same way.

After seeing the movement of the rope-span out in the middle of the river, Maura and Colleen were not interested in crossing. Erin would have done so with his father, but James felt it best to leave all the glory to the Allbees. Eliza was the first woman and Elbert the first child to cross the magnificent Mississippi River on a railroad bridge. The Kanes congratulated them and kept the secret of their crossing of the big bridge.

Chapter 21
MOVED
Saturday, 29 March 1856

Work on the railroad bridge moved along now with no more interruptions. The moveable span was completed while James' crew was laying the ties and spiking in the track on the stationary spans.

At home, James was more and more dissatisfied with where they were living. It was too close to the tracks in Rock Island, with the dirt and noise of trains passing day and night. He had been looking for a place in Davenport now that he was back on the payroll of the C&RI Railroad and also working at the newspaper. Maura gave him no argument because dusting in her small house, especially on warm days when the door and windows were open, was non-ending. She also was afraid that the hot cinders from the coal-burning trains might ignite their house.

So at the end of March 1856, the Kanes moved across the bridge at night using a horse and wagon borrowed from the Gannons. Though barricades were set up at either end of the bridge, with notices of penalties if people violated the notices, James had gotten permission from authorities to use it. For this one night, the swingspan was left closed for his convenience. The horse needed to be guided along the track, and Tom Gannon skillfully drove the horse and wagon across.

All of their belongings fit into the back of the wagon, along with Colleen, Erin and Sean, who had come to help. James and Maura sat on the seat in front with Tom. Moonlight helped them to avoid construction tools on the moveable span. Tom stopped the team at the Davenport exit so that James could move over the wooden barricade and then move it back after the wagon passed through.

James felt a great sense of relief once on ground again. He directed Tom to go beside the track and past the Davenport train depot. They moved toward town and two-thirds of the way up the hill to the house that James had found for his family. Since it was dark and they were all tired, they tied the horses to the post and went inside the house to rest on the floor till early morning, when they would unload and Tom could return to Rock Island before the workmen started their day.

Celebrating the completion of the new railroad bridge

111

Chapter 22
FINISHED
Tuesday, 22 April 1856

The Kanes had been in their new house for only three weeks when, on the 21st of April, the bridge was finished for a test run. The locomotive Fort Des Moines bravely crossed the wooden flat-top span from Rock Island, while three other new locomotives – the Nebraska, Iowa City and Kansas – followed, testing the bridge's endurance and strength. The next day a passenger train crossed the great river for the first time, with Henry Farnam as one of the passengers.

Although it was a big event for the railroad and the general citizenry, steamboat interests in Davenport, Rock Island and as far away as St. Louis were more than upset. "Stop the Bridge" clubs in St. Louis were popular.

"Ever since the bridge was started over two years ago, riverboat people have opposed it. Talk in the area has been anti-bridge by those who make their livelihood from steamboats," said Tom. "They think the bridge will cause river commerce to cease and their means of supporting themselves to disappear. For that reason, the celebration after the bridge was completed was purposely toned down by the railroad so as not to arouse more resentment."

The joy that men like Antoine LeClaire and Henry Farnam felt at having completed the bridge was tempered by the animosity of the riverboat men.

Tom Gannon was on hand as a reporter to write in the 22 April 1856 special edition of the *Davenport Gazette*. "It is the first day of a new era," he wrote. "Now Iowa City and many points west can be reached in hours instead of days. The first passenger train that crossed today has linked the Chicago and Rock Island Railroad to the Missouri and Mississippi Line, now forming one railroad, 'The Chicago Rock Island and Pacific Railroad.' Already the railroad is headed across Iowa toward Council Bluffs. The 'Calico Road' is being completed as you read." Then Tom explained the meaning of that nickname to the readers, having been privileged himself to that information from James Kane. He wanted to use James's name but thought better of it. He called them "the dedicated men who braved the heat and the cold in Indian territory to lay the track, only to be paid with bolts of calico."

Tom concluded, "After all the planning and preparation, hopes and disappointments, time spent in court and waiting for court decisions, this 'Work-of-Wonder' is done. The Mississippi River, that gigantic barrier, is spanned, allowing for the country to move westward."

But the Rock Island Railroad knew its enemies were close and didn't want a big celebration. However, it could not stop the church bells from ringing, and crowds from gathering on both shores to cheer. Fifty Sauk and Fox Indians watched from the Antoine LeClaire property in Davenport. People in the East learned of the event almost immediately by telegraph and were already looking forward to the next step, the train's arrival at the Pacific coast.

The Kanes were among the loudest celebrants. Each member had his or her reason for rejoicing. It was both sad and joyful for James. The bridge's completion marked an end to his career of laying railroad track, something for which he was proud. He was happy to have been a part of it.

Maura was proud of the part that James had had in the bridge, but was delighted to have it completed. She felt that he was now in a safer, steadier, and warmer type of work as a printer. Yes, she was very happy.

Erin had spent over two years watching the bridge rise out of the water and grow into the white beauty that it was. He knew many of the workers, and saw its progress daily. It was as though it was "his" bridge. He had drawn a picture of the bridge and mounted it on a stick to wave as he shouted his "Hurrahs."

The bridge had played a big part in Colleen's growing up, so Colleen, too, felt nostalgic. She had lived next to it in Rock Island, her father had laid its track, her brother had talked constantly about its progress, and her dearest friend had reported about it. It was wonderful to be finished, but she couldn't help feeling a little sad. The Rock Island Railroad Bridge was complete. She gave a big "Hurrah! Hurrah!" with tears in her eyes.

Chapter 23
THE *EFFIE AFTON*
Tuesday, 6 May 1856

Maura was very happy to be in her new one-and-a-half-story home. It was like heaven to be away from the train tracks and all the cinders; however, Harrison Street on which they now lived was not free from dust. It was often called "Ditch Street," because it was a ditch 20 feet wide. Rain ran down the dirt hill, making it a lovely mud slide, and in dry weather it was a very dusty track.

She now had a cast-iron parlor stove that James had bought "on credit" to heat the house. It was black with a silver-colored fancy skirt below the fire-door and a broad, bulbous top. It stood on four thin feet. Open vents in the upstairs floor allowed the heat to rise throughout the bedrooms, but that heat barely took the edge off of bitterly cold nights.

Erin and Colleen each had their own rooms now and Colleen still used the screen her parents had made for her in Rock Island, to section off a part of her room for writing. She had a small table as a desk, with a chair, and a window behind for lots of daylight. No one could be happier. Her father had painted the room pink, her favorite color, and stenciled one wall with butterflies in three sizes. She had drawn and cut them out of oiled paper for him to paint through. He used a little more red pigment in the paint to make the flying insects stand out yet remain delicate. Colleen herself added decorations to the wings. After the wall was complete, Colleen knew that it was better than the wallpaper she initially had hoped for.

Erin's room was small, with space only for a bed and chest of drawers. He didn't plan to spend time in it except to sleep, so nothing special was done. Maura chose a light yellow color of paint to make it cheerful and look larger.

The activity in Davenport seemed to have doubled from what the Kanes were used to in Rock Island, just across the river. Now they were in the center of a growing town. In 1836, Davenport had only 100 residents; but by 1850, when the Kanes arrived in Rock Island, Davenport had had a population of 1,848 and now, only six years later, according to the 1856 census that James read in the *Davenport Gazette*, there are 11,000 people in town. James knew that his family had increased the numbers by four. They were doing their part in a town growing by leaps and bounds.

Packet boats of people who either were relatives of local residents or adventurers looking for excitement or gold out west came regularly from St. Louis and St. Paul. Then there were the Irish and German immigrants looking for work and coming from the east by one of three ways of transportation: by boat down the Ohio River and up the Mississippi; by stagecoach, which was far less expensive and still flourishing in 1856; or by train, which took only three days from the east coast, as opposed to 18 days by other land means.

Downtown had been lighted by gaslights for the past two years. The dirt streets were lined with places of business – a tobacco store run by James Burge; three hotels – the Pennsylvania House, the Scott House, and the finest being the LeClaire House; a telegraph office; and a daguerreotype studio. O.L. Burdick had the studio since 1851, after which three others opened up.

Then there was a tailor shop, Wilson's Ferry Landing, a bakery on Front Street and Second, many carpenter shops, eight cigar stores that Erin counted, two furrier stores, millinery and dress-making shops, a nursery selling plants and shrubs, and a piano store that advertised in the newspaper regularly, blacksmith shops and numerous taverns.

In addition, there were watch and jewelry stores, soap and candle shops, upholstery places, an undertaker, and physicians. Dr. E.S. Burrows, being the first and only one for a year and a half, had also been active in founding the town.

Before 1856 every household in Davenport was prepared with two fire-buckets for water in case they were needed. The first real fire engine arrived after the Kanes moved from Rock Island. It caused Erin to change his grown-up goal from being a steamboat captain to becoming a fireman.

For eighteen years, St. Anthony's Church had been the only Catholic church in Davenport. Now in honor of his wife, Marguerite, Antoine LeClaire built another Catholic Church on top of the hill the same year that the Kanes moved to Davenport. It was called St. Margaret's, with Father Andrew Trevis, a Frenchman, as pastor. The Kanes chose to attend St. Margaret's from the time it was dedicated, in October.

Whenever the Gannons came for a visit in their horse and wagon, Tom would take the children for a ride to see the town. There was the unusual octagonal house on LeClaire Street, as well as Antoine LeClaire's mansion, above 7th Street, a delightful vision, with its porches and lookout tower. One of these tours, but with the adults along, took them to Burrows' palatial 30-room house northwest of Davenport, called "Clifton." Also on that ride they saw the German immigrants' cultural building "Turnverein," or "Turners," as it became known, about a block up from the river on the west side.

The new bridge was always a favorite place to visit. It was a destination of every tour, either at the beginning or end, and, if a train were crossing, it was especially exciting. The bridge was private property and only trains were allowed by law to use it. However, some citizens would cross when no train was expected and the bridge-tender, who lived on the extended pier below the turnspan, was not visible.

Just fifteen days after the bridge was completed, an event happened that would affect the lives of the townspeople for months and even years to come. A new packet boat, called the *Effie Afton*, came up from St. Louis on the fourteenth day carrying passengers, freight and mail. On leaving the Rock Island riverbank early the next morning, the Afton backed into the local ferryboat, the *Davenport*. Though both boats suffered only slight damage, the pilot of the *Effie Afton* continued in haste to catch up to and pass a sternwheeler, the *J.B.Carson*, already in the channel headed for the drawspan. The *Afton* passed the *Carson* and headed at an angle into the open bridge span on the Illinois side. The pilot lost control between the bridge piers and the *Afton* struck the small Rock Island pier. She careened into the long center pier and then back into the eastern pier, where she became stuck. Three fires started on the boat and passengers fled the quickly spreading flames by climbing onto the bridge and then fleeing to the island. The *J.B.Carson* steamed into the treacherous current, tied up and rescued the remaining passengers before the *Afton* became a raging inferno. Fire caught the first span of the bridge and eventually released the boat, which floated down to Credit Island and sank.

When the burning span of the bridge fell, steamboats from both sides of the river blew their whistles – either to warn other vessels or perhaps to celebrate that this impediment to their river travel had been partially destroyed.

Bad news like this travels fast. James, on this Tuesday, was discussing work opportunities with Antoine LeClaire when the news arrived. Antoine LeClaire jumped up immediately and hurried to the front porch, where the view of the river was unimpeded. The smoke and flames were visible. The second boat was in the process of rescuing the victims. He and James hastily climbed into his waiting buggy and LeClaire, with James beside him, raced to the scene. Naturally a large crowd had gathered and there was worry that the whole bridge would burn, so not too many people were brave enough to go out as far as James and LeClaire did. The spectators who were already there made way for LeClaire to pass to the bridge end. By this time the *Effie Afton* had already broken loose and was headed downstream. It was a sad sight. The bridge tender was anxiously throwing buckets of water on the swingspan as flying fiery debris threatened to set that part of the bridge on fire. He was able to prevent that from happening. His wife was also watching and ready by their brick house on the center elongated pier with his boat if a quick evacuation were needed. It wasn't necessary.

At home that evening, James and the whole family felt badly about the accident, but, for the sake of the children, the parents tried to be positive. "The bridge will be repaired and life will go on," said James. "No one was killed and the bridge was not a total loss. One span is gone from the fire, with its twisted track still hanging and another span damaged. The drawspan suffered no fire injury, thanks to Mr. Dray, the bridgetender. Some treatment should be given to the whole bridge to make it fireproof. That, I am sure, the railroad will consider." In analyzing the facts, James was making himself feel a little better. He would eventually be given more work because of the accident, but the cause did not make him happy.

When the children were upstairs in bed and out of earshot, James told Maura that he was concerned about all the joy the steamboat people seemed to have gotten from the affair. He told her about the whistles and revelry from the other boats. She said that she had heard it, but thought that some new steamboat had just arrived and they were greeting it. Then she saw the black smoke in the direction of the bridge.

Now the question arises: Was today's incident really an accident? James didn't even want to think such a thing.

Within a day of the incident the owners of the Effie Afton filed suit against the Railroad Bridge Company for damages. Because of the local navigation interests, the railroad prepared to fight the lawsuit in the United States Circuit Court rather than in the lower court. Knowing that a strong and popular man was needed to win this case, Norman Judd, the regular lawyer for the railroad, recommended a lawyer from Springfield, Abraham Lincoln. Though not yet widely recognized in 1856, Lincoln was known as a powerful lawyer. He was engaged to represent the railroad.

While all of this was going on, the Railroad began almost immediately to rebuild, barges carried the trains across the river, and by the 6th of September 1856, the first locomotive went across the rebuilt bridge. By the 17th of September, the bridge was in full service.

The Gannon's rocking horse

Chapter 24
RESTORED
Wednesday, 6 August 1856

Life changed for the Kanes after the *Effie Afton* accident. James was quite vocal in defending the railroad but many of his neighbors, coming from riverboat backgrounds, felt that the bridge was a river nuisance and should be torn down. This caused a coolness on the part of many toward the Kane family. In the public school, the children were sometimes left out of activities. Erin clung to his friendship with Sean Gannon, another defender of the bridge.

The Gannon family recently had moved to Davenport, for several reasons: the bridge was completed, there were numerous work opportunities, their friends the Kanes were there, and Tom Gannon now was working in Davenport. They found a brick house on the top of the hill on Main Street. It was a beauty and had many nice features – a kitchen sink with a water pump, corner windows in some bedrooms, fireplaces, and elegant draperies on the parlor, library and dining room windows. Maura had just one moment of jealousy, but then forgot it because she was happy with her own situation. She was truly happy for the Gannons, as well.

Sean, age 12, and Erin, nearly 10, discussed the bridge happenings when they got together. "I hope the railroad wins the lawsuit," commented Erin when the two met one day. "Have you thought what would happen to the bridge if they lost?" Erin, the serious one, had given this much consideration. "It would stop the movement west, at least temporarily. Someone would have to invent another way to cross the river besides boats. Maybe I'd think of a way to fly across." He had thoughts like this when he was alone and shared them today with his best friend. Sean just laughed and shoved his friend inside. "Come and see my brothers' toy," Sean said. It was a wooden horse with a wooden saddle on long wooden rockers. The boys had a good time testing it out – seeing who could rock the fastest, until Sean's younger brothers, Frankie and John, came into the room and protested that Erin and Sean were too big. With onlookers, Sean and Erin were glad to leave.

Next, they played checkers, which Sean won most of the time, until Mr. Gannon announced that they were going for a carriage ride to see the progress on the bridge reconstruction. In the last three months as many as 150 men had worked on the bridge at one time so that it was almost ready for use. In fact, the last work to be done was the laying of the track, and James Kane was in charge of that. Erin had heard his father talking about the progress, but living much farther away now, he had not seen how close the crews were to being finished. In the meantime, the trains were being ferried across the river to keep their schedules.

The scene no longer had the odor of burnt wood. Although the entrance to the bridge was blocked for vehicles, Mr. Gannon said they could walk out to the turnspan, which was left open for boat use when the workers didn't need it closed for their equipment to cross. The small group walked next to the track mostly, but Erin and Sean tried to stay on the steel itself, which was getting rusty from lack of use. From the gate at the end of the Iowa third span they could see the other end and the work that was done. A whole new span had been built and part of the last span on the island side that had been charred as well. Mr. Gannon said, "It appears that the only things missing are the ties and the track." Erin was anxious to get home to tell his father.

Chapter 25
THE LIBRARY
September 1856

Colleen loved books and very soon discovered the W. H. Holmes Bookstore. Mr. Holmes had been in business since 1850 and was well thought of by those who frequented his shop. Mr. Holmes sold notepads for 5 cents, as well as stationery and envelopes for mailing letters. In the past, Colleen's mother said that she had just folded the paper, after writing, and addressed the outside. Envelopes were something rather new. Since Colleen had no money to spend, she browsed.

Mr. Holmes knew, when he saw Colleen come in, that there would probably be no sale, but he liked the girl and didn't mind her visits. One day, after months of her visits, he said, "Did you know that there is a library now open where you can sit and read their books for free? For a small fee you can even take books home for a time!"

This was a wonderful revelation to Colleen. The library was known as the "Young Men's Literary Group" because men were the ones mostly interested, at the time, in furthering their knowledge, and this was the reason Mr. Holmes had not thought to tell her before. Besides, the literary group was Mr. Holmes's competition, you might say, and he was not out to promote his competition, but he did want to encourage the young girl's love of books.

Colleen set out the very next day to find the library. It was a single room in the Forrest Building on 4th and Brady streets into which her former house in Rock Island would fit four times. It seemed very large to her and the walls were lined with books. Other racks stood side by side in the middle of the room. Several tables with chairs for eight people filled the rest of the space. The librarian, an older man with white hair and spectacles, sat at a special desk opposite the door.

As Colleen entered, she was awestruck. She had never seen so many books and people quietly reading. It took her eyes a few minutes to adjust to the darkness before she went up to the man obviously in charge. "My name is Colleen Kane," she said, as she nervously stood before him. "I love to read and I just found out about your library."

"Good afternoon, Miss Kane," he responded with a twinkle in his eye. "I am Mr. Hundgate, the librarian. I'm so glad you found us. Yes, we have over one thousand books and journals on all different subjects and you can come and read them anytime. If you wish to borrow a book and take it home, we have two methods. You can join with a monthly fee or pay per book."

With his last statement, Colleen's face fell. She had no money and she knew her folks had a hard time making ends meet. But Mr. Hundgate said she could read the books at the library for free. "Oh, yes, I would love that," said Colleen.

After school, when she was done with her chores on Saturdays, and almost daily during the summer, Colleen visited the library. She became very familiar with Nathaniel Hawthorne's fables – *The Golden Touch*, *The Three Golden Apples*, *The Miraculous Pitcher* and many more.

Then she read *Gulliver's Travels*, by Jonathan Swift, and *Alice in Wonderland*, by Lewis Carroll, and these reinforced her desire to be a writer.

Her favorite thing of all was to look through Godey's *Lady's Book*, a monthly journal that had beautiful pictures of the latest fashions in clothes, hair styles and accessories, plus charming love stories for women.

Colleen truly enjoyed what the reading room had to offer and Mr. Hundgate enjoyed having her visit. They became friends.

One day Colleen arrived especially enthusiastic and sat down with Daniel Defoe's *Robinson Crusoe*. As she read, all she could think of was Erin and how much he would like this book. However, she knew she didn't have the 5 cents to take it home. When she was leaving, she told the librarian her feelings. "My brother would really like this book. I wish I had the fee to take it home."

Mr. Hundgate looked around and spoke very quietly to Colleen. "Bright Eyes," as he called her, "You are so faithful and responsible that I think I can let you take this book home as long as you see that nothing happens to it."

"But I don't have the 5 cents," she objected.

"I know, but the fee is mostly to make sure the books are returned. I know you and know that I don't need to be concerned about that. So I am saying that you can borrow the book without the fee." Secretly he planned to put the money into the "kitty" himself.

Colleen was so happy and surprised that almost without thinking she jumped up and gave him a peck on the cheek and drew the book close to her chest with both hands. "Oh, thank you so much! I will take good care of it and return it when we are through. I'll read it to Erin before bed. I know he'll love it."

"Bright Eyes, you can keep it until you are done unless someone asks for it. Then I'll have to have you return it."

"Mr. Hundgate, you are an angel! Thank you! Thank you!" With that, Colleen left the reading room and ran home while hugging the treasure with one hand and her hat with the other.

That night she told Erin she had a surprise for him. He was used to going to bed at eight o'clock on school nights but it was summer and eight-thirty or nine was his bedtime. Colleen, now 14, usually was up a half hour longer. However, tonight she went upstairs with Erin and took him to her room, where she had laid the book on her desk. "Mr. Hundgate let me take this book home to read it to you," she explained. "It's about a boy your age who is shipwrecked and lives on an island alone for years."

Erin, an adventurous soul, was intrigued and Colleen read by candlelight until his head was nodding.

Chapter 26
JOHN DEERE
Wednesday, 8 October 1856

John Deere was a name known by all local farmers in 1856 because they bought his plows, which were made in Moline, slightly east across the river from Davenport. John Deere plows were perfect for the Midwest land because Deere used steel in his machines that allowed the earth's clay to roll off instead of sticking to the plow. Urban citizens in the area were aware of Deere because he advertised in the *Davenport Daily Gazette* and the *Rock Island Republican* newspapers, which contained a picture of his product. John Deere lived in a lovely home on a hill in Moline with a view of the river and of his factory.

Tom Gannon, always looking out for the possibility of a news story, overheard some men talking about Davenport's postmaster. "Antoine LeClaire was out late last night. He in his horse and buggy came flying down the street, kicking up the dry dirt as he went. It awakened me and my wife as he yelled at his horse. It must have been something important." That was all Tom needed to hear. He knew he must find Mr. LeClaire.

Hunting for LeClaire and knowing that the morning train was due at 10 a.m. with the mail, Tom headed for the depot. LeClaire would probably be there to pick up the mailbag. He always sorted the letters and put them in his large pockets for delivery throughout the day around town.

Tom was correct. LeClaire was there with his buggy, patting and lovingly talking to his white horse while wiping the animal down. With his great weight and size, LeClaire did not bend down, but only got the parts of the horse he could reach while standing.

"Mr. LeClaire, I'm Tom Gannon with the *Davenport Gazette*. I understand you were out late last night," he began.

Antoine LeClaire, being a tall man, looked down at Tom for a second and continued his efforts for the animal. "That is true, Mr. Gannon – may I call you Tom? Something potentially tragic happened at the bridge and was called to my attention." He then proceeded to tell Tom a story that made his hair stand on end.

LeClaire said, "Last evening, John Deere had been in Davenport for a sales promotion in the LeClaire House with farmers from the surrounding areas. The farmers' crops were mostly in and they had an evening free to come to see what was new for the coming season. It was a dinner meeting and the usually bib-overalled men were squirming in their best dress.

"By nine-thirty the last of the guests had left and John Deere wanted to wind down before heading for home. It was a beautiful harvest-moon evening as Deere and his manager from the plant were walking by the end of the newly repaired bridge. Immediately, they noticed three men bent over on the bridge, moving something around. As Deere told me, these men didn't seem to be crossing, or standing, or admiring the beauty of the moon reflected on the water. They looked like they were up to no good, so Deere yelled, 'Hey there, what are you doing?'"

"At the sound of John Deere's voice, the three stood up and jumped into a waiting boat and rowed away, disappearing into the night.

"Deere and his friend hurried to the spot on the bridge just vacated and found piles of dry brush, rags and a volatile liquid the three men had left. Their hearts raced as they realized that they had foiled a plot to burn the bridge. Mr. Dray, the bridgetender, came down the bridge from his control spot when he saw all the commotion. He took the evidence to his residence on the elongated pier for safe-keeping.

"Before ferrying across the river, Deere informed me at home, since I live up the hill only a short distance."

The next day the following article appeared on the second page of the newspaper.

JOHN DEERE STOPS BRIDGE FIRE

By Thomas Gannon

Thanks to one of our esteemed local citizens, another tragedy was averted on our new bridge. Two nights ago, John Deere and a friend were passing the Davenport end of the Chicago and Rock Island Railroad Bridge when they viewed something strange going on. About 50 feet away, on the bridge, three men were bent over something. Despite the moonlit night, John Deere could not tell exactly what it was, but he called out, demanding to know what they were up to. Caught in the act, they immediately got away by boat. It was discovered that they had left behind rags, branches, flammable liquid and an evil intent. That evidence is now being held by Fred Dray, the bridgetender.

Local townspeople and the Chicago and Rock Island

Railroad are most grateful to John Deere, a man well-known throughout the region for his farm plow business in Moline, for preventing another fire on the only railroad bridge that crosses the Mississippi River. When the Effie Afton hit the span earlier this year and caused it to catch on fire, the bridge was out of commission for four months. This caused not only a great financial burden for the railroad but delays and frustrations for those people headed for the Western towns and prairies.

John Deere is a regular advertiser in this newspaper.

It was Colleen who first saw the article when she was looking at the newspaper in the reading room. She was more excited to see Tom's name attached than at the news the article conveyed. This was not his first by-line by any means, but still it caused her great pride to know the author of an article in the newspaper. They had been friends for over two years and at age 14, she was beginning to feel differently about Tom. Boys at school were so immature, she felt. Tom was older, taller, handsome and a writer like she wanted to be. He was also gentle, kind, and knowledgeable. When she said stupid things, he didn't laugh but found something reasonable in it.

Colleen was so excited to read about the incident that she had to speak to someone. The librarian was at his desk busy doing some recording when she came up. "Mr. Hundgate, did you hear about what happened two nights ago?" began Colleen. "My friend, Tom Gannon, wrote the story in the *Gazette*. Some evil men tried to burn down the bridge!"

Mr. Hundgate had heard from friends about the damage averted, but had not read it in the paper as yet. But for Colleen, he played ignorant. "No, Bright Eyes, is that right? Tell me about it!"

Colleen proceeded to describe what she had just read about John Deere and the potential arsonists who got away. "Tom just wrote about it, but if he had been there, they would not have gotten away," she added.

Hearing this last part, Mr. Hundgate encouraged her to elaborate on this 'knight in shining armor.' "Who is this Tom?" he asked.

For Mr. Hundgate's benefit, Colleen went back to when she met Tom in church in Rock Island, to seeing him at work when he just set type while going to high school, and then explained that now he is a full-time reporter here in Davenport and that he and his family have visited her house and vice versa.

Just at that moment, Tom Gannon walked into the library. He was writing an article on the presidential election that was coming up in November and wanted to research the life of James Buchanan and his opponent. Franklin Pierce had not been a very strong or inspiring leader for the last four years and Tom wanted to present a story about the possibility of someone who could inspire the country and deal with the racial issue that was now an cause of great divisiveness.

Tom greeted Colleen warmly and was introduced to the librarian. He was a member of the reading room but never had time before to meet or talk to Mr. Hundgate. They discussed the newspaper article, and Mr. Hundgate complimented Tom for his by-line, and agreed that some riverboat people would have been happy if the bridge did burn down. A man came to the desk, then, needing Mr. Hundgate's assistance, which ended the conversation.

Colleen and Tom in the Reading Room

131

Chapter 27
POLITICS
Thursday, 9 October 1856

Tom went back to the political section of books in the room and began his digging. Colleen, having nothing especially pressing to read, offered to help him. Together they found everything written about the candidates.

"This fall is election year, I know. Papa talks about it sometimes and Mamma is unhappy that she can't vote," commented Colleen.

"Who does your father favor?" asked Tom as he pulled down a recent journal from the stacks.

"He thinks that James Buchanan, the Democratic candidate, has the most experience. He says Buchanan was a U.S. Senator, Secretary of State under Polk, and has been until recently Minister to England. He has never married, so Papa says he has no distractions, which Mamma objects to hearing."

Maybe I should interview your father," said Tom. "He sounds like he knows more than most people."

"He wants to see our government be the best it can be. He is so glad to be free of the oppression he felt in Ireland. He reads all that he can and talks to anyone who knows about politics." Colleen was very proud of her father.

Tom spread the material out on one of the reading room tables and the two of them started to read and take notes. Colleen chose James Buchanan to research and Tom had John Charles Fremont, the Republican.

Colleen found in a journal that Buchanan was running on a "Save the Union" theme. He personally opposed slavery, but had taken the middle ground to maintain peace. As Colleen's father had told her, Buchanan had had an honorable record of 40 years of public service in both state and federal offices. He held three fundamental beliefs, according to the article: (1) that compromise was the only way for the federal government to survive; (2) that citizens had to obey the law even if they thought it unjust; and (3) that questions of morality could not be settled by political action. Slavery was the big issue in the country and Buchanan would do anything to prevent a civil war.

On a personal level, Colleen found that, at one time, Buchanan was engaged to the daughter of a wealthy ironmaster. Her family disapproved and even accused him of fortune-hunting. A number of incidents led to the breaking of the engagement, and a week later she died. The article said, "It could possibly have been suicide." After that, Buchanan never married.

Tom found that Fremont, the Republican candidate, was called the "Pathfinder" because from 1840 to 1846 he led an expedition to help open up the West. He became Governor of the new California Territory in January 1847, and then from 1850 to 1851 was U.S. Senator from California. He became rich when gold was struck on his land in California. Early on he was in the military in Georgia and became strongly anti-slavery.

His father-in-law, Senator Benton, a Democrat, opposed his son-in-law's candidacy. Tom had even heard people say, "Why would anyone want to vote for Fremont when his own father-in-law would not?" Another article stated that some of Fremont's violently anti-slavery supporters wanted a Northern withdrawal from a Union that allowed slaveholders.

Exhausting his sources on Fremont, Tom began research on Millard Fillmore, who was running again on the "Know-Nothing" or American ticket. He had been the 13th President, just before Pierce, but he was trying a comeback as a "Know-Nothing" candidate.

Colleen, having finished her research, looked over Tom's shoulder and asked, "What is the Know-Nothing Party?"

Tom had heard of them often during the present administration. "Colleen, when President Pierce chose his cabinet, he appointed James Campbell from Pennsylvania as Postmaster General. Campbell was the first Catholic ever to hold such an office, and the same year the papal nuncio, Monsignor Gaetano Bedini, visited America. These combined events raised an anti-Catholic outburst and brought the new party into being, called the Know-Nothings or American Party."

"You mean there is a political party that is basically anti-Catholic?" asked Colleen, unbelieving.

"Some people are afraid of what they don't know, Colleen," replied Tom philosophically. "They think the Pope will come over here and take over. But it isn't only Catholics, but the Irish, the Masons and maybe more that the Know-Nothings are against."

Tom went back to his research on President Fillmore. He found that Fillmore was born in a log cabin in a county in New York in 1800, and rose from there to wealth and the White House when he was 50. He worked on his parents' farm, went to a one-room schoolhouse and later married his red-headed former school teacher. He became a lawyer in 1823 and moved to Buffalo seven years later. As a Whig he held a state office and was a U.S. Representative in the House for eight years before becoming Vice President under Zachary Taylor. But Taylor died the following year and Fillmore became President. Fillmore favored the "Compromise of 1850," written by Henry Clay as a solution to the slavery issue. It did not pass as a single bill, but was broken up into five bills, written by Senator Stephen A. Douglas, as follows:

1. Admit California as a free state
2. Pay Texas to abandon her claims to New Mexico
3. Make New Mexico a territory
4. Provide Federal agents to help slaveholders to find fugitives
5. Abolish slave trade in the District of Columbia

These each got a majority vote in the Senate and each was signed by President Fillmore. The bills were not a solution to slavery, but a tentative truce.

However, it was the "Fugitive Slave Act" that Fillmore signed into law that denied him a nomination in 1852. Could he do better now, just four years later? Would people remember?

Tom and Colleen left the library much better-informed citizens than they were a few hours before. They both knew for whom each would have voted, if they could have.

Tom tried to write his article to be factual and unbiased. But in this case it was those facts that defeated Fillmore and elevated Buchanan. In November, Buchanan received 174 electoral votes, to Fremont's 114, and Fillmore's 8. Tom and Colleen were happy.

Another political event of the fall had occurred when the Republican Party of Davenport invited Abraham Lincoln to come to speak. Tom Gannon was informed of the invitation and had written an article for the *Gazette* with the headlines, "Springfield Lawyer Invited to Davenport." Before election time, Mr. Lincoln responded that he was preparing for the Rock Island Railroad lawsuit and might be able to combine a research trip and the talk. Although the Republicans had hoped to boost their candidates with an appearance by the well-known and popular Lincoln prior to the election, the presentation never occurred.

So ended 1856, with James Buchanan as the President-elect, slavery a big issue throughout the country, and the longevity of the new bridge still in question.

Chapter 28
CAPTAIN HARRIS
Monday, 23 March 1857

The Mississippi River was not dependable and could be a formidable foe.

Just about 200 feet above the Chicago and Rock Island Railroad Bridge were the Rock Island Rapids, as they were called. "It is the most dangerous part of the whole Mississippi River," said many pilots. "The river twists and turns around chains of rocks that protrude from the shores on both sides. These rocks fill the river for fifteen miles upstream having been left there from the glacier period. River pilots who are familiar with the area could run the rapids with some degree of safety, but, those who are not shouldn't try."

LeClaire, Iowa, a town at the head of the rapids, was home to at least 20 of these experienced pilots. When large boats arrived from the north, these skilled men would board the vessel and navigate it through the treacherous waters down to Davenport and Rock Island. If the river was low, cargoes were loaded into flatboats known as "lighters." These lighters were pulled over the rapids by horses or oxen. This was very expensive, $50 a trip, as compared to 20 to 30 cents a bushel normally. Sometimes the water was so low that goods had to be stored or taken around the rapids by wagon. Sometimes in winter ice might close it for up to five months and if there was a dry summer, there was no telling how long the river might be unnavigable.

Among the "rescue pilots" living in LeClaire was Captain Daniel Smith Harris. If there were an organization or union of pilots at the time, he would have been president. He was the first to open up the navigation season by bringing his boats into port first in the spring. He was last to leave in the fall.

The *War Eagle* was the pride of Captain Harris and had been the fastest on the upper Mississippi River until 1850. Now he was about to launch the *Grey Eagle*. It was for this inaugural trip that Harris had come to Davenport.

Erin and Sean were in the general store, getting some small supplies for Erin's mother, when they saw an elegant-looking man coming in. He was tall, straight, very confident-looking, in rich clothes the likes of which the boys had never seen before. He had a ruffled blue shirt front, high silk hat, kid gloves and many diamonds, along with a very expensive, stylish tan suit for this beautiful spring day. The boys didn't know who he was until the owner addressed him as "Captain Harris." Erin whispered, "He is king of the river." The Captain was out to buy personal supplies of tobacco and liquor for his trip north to open the river to navigation for the 1857 season.

"Captain, don't you think it is a little early to be going north?" asked Mr. Klindt, the storekeeper. "There are still large ice floes on the river here. Up by Lake Pepin and north it must be pretty solid." But Captain Harris answered with certainty, "By the time I arrive in that area, the ice will have broken up. There will be no problems." He paid and was out the door.

All this time the boys were standing by the candy counter, but it wasn't the candy that interested them. Captain Harris had held their attention as though they were hypnotized. The two looked at each other as he left and then ran to the door to see where he went. However, Captain Harris had turned around to return, having remembered something that he needed. The boys and he collided just inside the heavy oak door. Erin was knocked to the floor, but Sean caught his balance and remained standing. Captain Harris was hardly flustered, having dealt with the unexpected on a daily basis. He reached to help Erin up and apologized for the accident. The storeowner came over and brushed the sawdust off Erin's clothes.

"Are you all right, lad?" Harris asked, quite concerned.

"I think so," replied Erin, not really sure of what happened. Then, "Thanks for the help," he said, remembering his manners. He was a little dazed. "Aren't you Captain Daniel Smith Harris?" he stammered, realizing what just took place.

"That is correct, lad, and what might your names be?" Harris replied, a little surprised as he looked down on the young boys for the first time.

"Erin James Kane, and this is Sean B. Gannon, my best friend," immediately stated Erin, thinking that middle names were important to this man, but not knowing what the "B" stood for in Sean's name.

"Well, Erin James Kane and Sean B. Gannon, it is nice to know you," he responded with a twinkle in his eye for the formality Erin had shown with their full names. He extended his hand to each and then continued, "Can I buy you some candy? It might make you feel a little better?" He knew he had caused the accident, but it was clearly difficult for him to humble himself.

"Oh, er, no, that isn't necessary. It really wasn't your fault. We wanted to see where you were going and were following you out the door when you came back in. It was just an accident," stammered Erin. Sean was still in awe of this man, but agreed with a little grunt and a nodding of his head.

"I have a better idea. How would you both like to see my new steamer, my *Grey Eagle?*"

With eyes almost popping out of their heads, Erin and Sean glanced at one another before looking back at Captain Harris to make sure he was serious. "I am on my maiden trip with this ship up to Lake Pepin and above to St. Anthony's Falls as soon as the ice lets up. She is a beauty and will be the fastest boat on the river like my *War Eagle* was in the past," Harris boasted.

Forgetting completely what he was in the store to do and the promises he had made to his parents in the past, Erin and Sean followed Captain Harris out of the store and down windy, cold Front Street. Where the boardwalk ended, there was only packed dirt and sand to walk on down an incline to the river's edge. The *Grey Eagle* stood alone at the cobblestone bank. If there were other steamers, the *Eagle* would have stood out with its shiny new black double-stacks, grey color, fancy silver and black trim and name prominently written on the side.

Today there was no problem finding it – rather, there was concern for its safety with the ice floes and rough water in the warm afternoon breeze. A crowd had gathered to see the first boat of the year. When Captain Harris and the boys arrived, the masses parted like the Red Sea to allow them to walk to the gangplank.

There were "Oh's" and "Ah's" at the sight of the pilot and his small entourage. Erin and Sean felt very special. On board, the deck hands greeted the captain and looked questioningly at the two boys, whom Captain Harris introduced as future captains. To 10-year-old Erin, this was very strange because that was exactly what he was thinking, "When I grow up, I think I'll be a riverboat captain."

Captain Harris had felt the same way when he was fifteen and saw the *Virginia* for the first time. He had been awestruck and set out to get enough money to buy his own boat. It was at the Galena lead mines in 1824, the next year, that he had found a rich vein of lead in a deserted shaft and got enough money to become a steamboat man with his brother. The admiring look in the boys' eyes was not hard to read.

Captain Harris took the boys from stem to stern on all three decks and into the hold and lower hold where the cargo of non-perishable food, tools and animals for the northern territories was stored. Many of these materials were things people had run out of during the winter. Families in Lake Pepin and St. Anthony, Minnesota, were anxiously awaiting their replenishment. "Everything smells new except the animals," commented Erin. Captain Harris was very pleased to show his "pride and joy" to anyone and bragged that it would outrun any boat on the upper Mississippi or any of its tributaries.

The galley had tables for the crew, and the captain had the cook serve the youngsters milk and cookies. Lastly, Captain Harris showed them his pilothouse and they pretended to steer the moored ship. They admired the view of Rock Island across the river, of the river itself with its fast-moving mainstream and chunks of white ice glowing in the afternoon sun, and the houses on the hill. Erin could even see his own house from this vantage point, which caused something inside of him to suddenly remember, "We should be home!"

It was getting late in the afternoon and that trip to the general store seemed so long ago. He still had the money for what his mother wanted him to buy. Erin's conscience screamed at him, "Your mother is worried about you. Get home now!"

Erin looked up at Captain Harris, who had been enjoying seeing the happiness on the boys' faces, but now Erin's expression had changed to fear. "What's the matter?" he asked as he touched Erin's shoulder.

"We have to go. Mamma sent me and my friend Sean to the store to get some molasses for beans she was fixing for supper. But when we bumped into to you, we forgot about it and then we came on your boat. That was hours ago and I know she is worried and I'm going to be in trouble."

With that rattled-off explanation, the boys turned and ran. But Erin turned around and yelled, "Thank you for the tour, Captain," almost running into a stevedore.

Captain Harris stood still, mouth open, looking after them. He liked the youngsters and didn't want to see them get into trouble. But what could he do to help?

Chapter 29
VISITOR
Monday, 23 March 1857

Maura was beside herself with worry. It had been about 1:00 o'clock when the boys left for the store. She knew that they might play along the way, but it was now 4:30. Something must have happened to them, she felt. Just as she herself was getting ready to go to the store to check, Erin and Sean came in panting, having run all the way from the boat.

They took turns explaining what had happened and apologized for worrying her. When she asked for the molasses, their heads dropped. They didn't have it. Erin produced the money.

Maura reprimanded Erin for not being more responsible and both of them for going with a stranger and 'onto a ship?' "Why, you could have been taken, kidnapped, put in a cargo hold and sold as slaves down the river." Maura was letting her imagination run wild, but she wanted to scare them into realizing how dangerous it was.

"But, Mamma, we were with Captain Harris. He's like king of the riverboat pilots and he wouldn't let anything happen to us," they argued.

"All the more reason for him to get by with anything – no one would question him. You did wrong by going with him. Now you both go upstairs and think about what you did."

She had to sit down for a minute when the boys were out of sight, to regain her composure. She was very shaken by the news of where they had been. Then she started supper and planned around the lack of molasses.

Erin and Sean had been home for about an hour. James and Colleen had arrived and were told of the boys' escapade. Then came a rap on the front door. Maura opened the door and before her stood a stately-looking man in a tall silk hat, tan suit and ruffled blue shirt.

"Mrs. Kane, I expect," he started. She nodded in response. "My name is Captain Daniel Smith Harris," and with that he bowed to her from the waist. "I met your son today and I wanted to confirm with you that he was not at fault for being late. It was my fault," he continued. "May I come in?"

Maura couldn't believe her eyes. She was stunned and unable to talk for a moment, but she did open the door for him. Regaining her composure, she said, "May the good Lord be with us! Yes, come in, come in."

141

With that, Maura escorted him into the sitting room and excused herself while she went to get James. James was in the kitchen, washing up in the wash basin with water he had heated on the wood stove. He was drying himself when he saw Maura in the doorway, looking quite pale and excited.

"James, you won't believe this but there is a riverboat captain in our sitting room. Captain Harris, that Erin met today, in all his finery, is in OUR house, sitting in OUR chair right at this moment. What am I supposed to do?"

James was calm, having met important people before, so he rather slowly and deliberately put on his clean shirt, buttoned it up, tucked it in at the waist and followed his wife to the front of the house.

Captain Harris had been looking around at the sparse furniture in this immaculately clean room. There were two solid high-back wooden chairs, two wooden stools obviously made by an amateur furniture maker and the most valuable piece, a spinning wheel with thread on it in progress. A small table held a candle in a metal holder and a wooden candle-box for storing a year's supply of candles was on the floor nearby.

He stood when James and Maura entered and offering his hand, he said, "Mr. Kane, I'm Captain Harris." His top hat lay on the table and in his hand he had a package which he handed to Maura. "This is what I believe you sent Erin to the store to buy that I caused him to forget." Then he proceeded to tell the same story that Erin had told his mother of the events of the afternoon. "I didn't want him to be punished for something that was my fault," he ended.

By this time, Erin and Sean heard an unusual voice downstairs and came to look. However, they couldn't see because the sitting room sliding door was closed. But the loud resonant voice was unmistakable – Captain Harris was here in Erin's house! Why had he come?

At that precise moment, the pocket-door slid open and Captain Harris, hat in hand, stepped into the hallway, followed by Maura and James. Seeing the sheepish-looking boys, he greeted them wholeheartedly.

"Sean and Erin, it is good to see you again!" Then, looking at Erin, he said, "I've met your wonderful parents. You are so lucky. Always do what they say and never give them cause to worry. I am sorry about this afternoon. I should have had you get permission before going on my *Grey Eagle*. But I think it is all ironed out now. I'll see you again the next time I'm coming through Davenport." With that and a handshake with James, and a bow to Maura, the captain left by the front door.

The boys were full of questions. How did he find the house? Did he follow them? What did Mamma and Papa think of him? What did he mean, I'll see you again? But it was time to eat and Colleen was in the kitchen with the meal ready and anxious to hear what was happening.

So over supper, the happy family discussed Captain Harris. When Erin told him that he forgot the molasses, the Captain knew where he could find out where the Kanes lived. "Mr. Klindt, at the General Store, may God be with him, told him. He bought the molasses you forgot, Erin. He also brought some bonbons which we can have for dessert."

James and Maura were very impressed with Captain Harris and Maura forgave the boys somewhat for giving her such a stressful afternoon. "We invited him to dinner but he said he would come another time. He has to prepare to leave for the north possibly tomorrow."

That night Erin dreamed of sailing with the Captain on the *Grey Eagle*. The Captain was sick and Erin had to take over steering the ship. There was a fog and he couldn't see where he was headed until all of a sudden a huge tree was in front of the boat. As they were about to hit it, Erin woke up in a cold sweat.

Chapter 30
ABRAHAM LINCOLN
Tuesday, 1 September 1857

Tuesday, the first of September, Tom and Colleen met at the Library after work and school. "What a beautiful day it has been, Tom! Wouldn't it be fun to have a picnic on the green by the river?" It was a spontaneous idea and something they had never done before. "It is too bad I didn't think of it before so I could have made some picnic fare."

"Oh, no," said Tom, "that would take all the fun out of it. Let's just go to the general store and the bakery and buy what we want." Saying that, Tom took Colleen's hand, and they headed for the store feeling very light-hearted and free. Colleen wasn't so sure what they could buy, but was willing to go along with whatever Tom wanted.

Once they were in the store, Tom headed for the barrel of apples. "Do you like apples?" he asked. When she nodded, he picked out two big rosy ones.

Next he asked the clerk what kind of cheese he had. "We have a wheel of Swiss cheese and cheddar," was the answer. Colleen had not had Swiss before, so he ordered several slices of each. Looking around a little more he decided that was all they needed from there. After paying the clerk, the happy pair turned to leave for the bakery and almost ran into Fred Dray, who was just entering the establishment.

"Mr. Dray, how nice it is to see you," remarked Tom.

Surprised, but pleased to see Tom, Mr. Dray responded, "Gannon, I have an exclusive for you. You do work for the *Davenport Daily Gazette*, do you not?"

Tom was taken aback with this announcement, nodded and quickly said, "Yes, of course! What do you have?"

"Well, I was in my office on the bridge today and a tall, thin, bushy-haired young man came in to see me. He said his name was Abraham Lincoln, counsel for the Rock Island Railroad, regarding the *Effie Afton* accident. He asked me questions: Where was I at the time? What did I see? What was the current like?"

"Wait, wait, wait! You say Abraham Lincoln stopped to see you today? You are sure it was him?" asked Tom, almost breathless.

"Yes, I'm positive. I have seen a poster of him with his bony-looking face. Besides, who else would be asking such questions? I don't know how much help I was to him, but I hope some. I thought you might be interested in knowing."

"I'm surprised it wasn't announced that he was coming. What time was that, Mr. Dray?" asked Tom as he glanced aside at Colleen with his eyes sparkling.

"Oh, I would say about 2:15 this afternoon."

"Do you think he might still be in town? Maybe I can interview him!"

"No, I don't think so. He spent from about 9:00 o'clock this morning until 1:30 going back and forth through the 'draw' with the two Smith Brothers and Silas Lancaster from LeClaire. He must have chartered their steamboat and hired them, all top-notch pilots, to get firsthand information about what the boat can and can't do when passing others and going through the drawspan. Then I saw him talking to Mr. Brayton, the bridge engineer, before he came to see me," Mr. Dray said.

"But maybe he is still around," argued Tom.

"No, he told me he was going to go back to Chicago at 5:00 o'clock, on the private railroad car that he came on. That train left half an hour ago. I'm sorry, Tom."

Tom was disappointed, but still very pleased to get all the information that Mr. Dray had to provide him. He had more questions for the bridge master.

"What did he do after he left you, Mr. Dray?"

"Well, I saw him go back on the island side of the bridge where the *Effie Afton* hit and the fire and damage were sustained. He wasn't there long when he started talking to young Benjamin Brayton, who spends a lot of time on the bridge watching the river. They both sat on the edge of the deck and watched the current flow. I know that young 'un. He is very bright, being the son of the bridge engineer, and comes around here a great deal. He knows more than most about the river."

"How old is the boy?"

"I'd say about fourteen or fifteen," answered Mr. Dray.

"How long did they talk?"

"They were there a good hour. I know because the 4:15 train came and they were still checking out something in the river."

That appeared to be the extent of the news Mr. Dray could provide. Tom thanked him profusely for letting him know about Lincoln, and he and Colleen left the store. As they left, all Tom could think about now was this news.

Colleen knew that they would need to postpone the picnic because Tom would want to interview some of the same people that Lincoln saw and write his article as soon as possible. She suggested that he take the food because he would probably be working late. She could walk home alone because there still was plenty of light.

Tom was grateful that she understood and apologized that they didn't have the picnic, which he assured her they would do another time. He gave her a kiss on the cheek when they parted at Harrison Street. This took away a little of the disappointment that she felt.

The big problem that Tom had at the moment was to find the Braytons'. He knew who might know where they lived – Antoine LeClaire. Tom needed speed so that no other reporter would get the news before he could report it. So he went immediately to his newspaper office to borrow a horse and ride to LeClaire's residence on the hill.

By the time he arrived, it was 6 o'clock and the family was curious as to why anyone would be gracing their doorway at this time of day.

"My name is Tom Gannon, a reporter for the *Davenport Daily Gazette*, Mr. LeClaire. I apologize for interrupting your evening meal, but I have a news story I'm working on and I need an address as soon as possible."

"Come in, Tom," Antoine said while extending his hand. "I'm glad to know you. I've seen you with the Kane family at times. What is it I can do for you?

Tom explained in a few sentences what Mr. Dray had told him. The mention of Abraham Lincoln made LeClaire perk up with wide open eyes. He offered Tom a seat in the front parlor. Tom sat down, but said that he was not going to be there long. "Lincoln was here all day; he just left on the 5:00 o'clock train to Chicago."

"How can it be that we were not informed of his coming?" wondered LeClaire. "The trial is scheduled for the 22nd of this month and he must have been researching the accident. I am disappointed we were not able to greet him. He would be recognized by people if he were in the regular passenger cars, so possibly the railroad company was trying to keep his visit quiet by giving him a private car to travel in. Probably that was wise, with the anti-bridge feeling around here."

"I am sorry, I am rattling on and you are in a hurry and had an address you wanted, Tom?"

Abraham Lincoln and Ben Brayton on the railroad bridge

149

"Yes, Mr. LeClaire, I would like the Brayton family address. Since the boy spoke to Lincoln for over an hour, I would like to find out what they discussed for my story. However, if what you were saying is true, and the railroad does not want it known that Lincoln was here, maybe this story should not be published. I have not told anyone else about it as yet."

"That is up to you, Tom. That is asking a lot for a reporter not to report a big news story like this. But the surprise element of the information that Lincoln learned while here might make a difference in the outcome of the lawsuit. I can give you the address of the Brayton family, however." With that, LeClaire checked his addresses for the exact number of the house.

"Thank you for whatever you decide to do, Tom. It has been nice to have met such an outstanding young man as you. I'll be watching the *Gazette* to see if the story appears. Good night!" With that, Mr. LeClaire held the door until Tom left.

Now Tom was in a quandary: should he write the story or not? The one thing he did know was that he wanted to talk to Benjamin Brayton, Jr. What he had to say might influence what should be done with the information. Tom looked at the address that Antoine LeClaire had given him. It was 10th and Harrison, just north of the Kane household. That was a surprise.

Tom had no trouble finding the Brayton house. It happened that the young Brayton boy was in the stable behind the house taking off the saddle from his horse, and hanging it on a two-by-four projecting from the wall. Tom rode up to the stable entry, got off his horse and introduced himself to young Ben.

"I understand that you talked to Abraham Lincoln today on the railroad bridge. Fred Dray, the bridgetender, told me he had seen you."

"Yes, that is true. I love to spend time on the river and on the bridge thinking, planning, watching trains and dreaming. Mr. Lincoln asked me if I knew how fast the river ran under the bridge. I told him that I had never thought of it, but we could figure it out."

"Mr. Lincoln asked you to tell him how?"

"I told him that we can sight logs and brush coming down the river. From where they swing out about 300 yards away we can see how long it takes until they swing in again under the bridge. Mr. Lincoln had a silver watch in his vest pocket which he used to do the timing. Then I spotted a log coming and told him when it swung out from the island. He observed the moment on his watch and stopped the time when the log reached the bridge. That gave us the distance and the time. Mr. Lincoln seemed happy with the outcome."

The boy was very matter-of-fact, Tom noted, and not too excited at having helped a big-time lawyer from Springfield perhaps preserve the very bridge he had been sitting on.

Tom thanked him and left.

It was still light and Tom was only three blocks away from Colleen's house, so he decided to stop. The whole Kane family was glad to see him, as always, but especially Erin, since Tom came on horseback. Erin loved all animals and petted the horse as it was hitched to the post.

Colleen and Tom went for a walk down to the river. He told Colleen about getting the Brayton address from LeClaire, and about speaking to Ben Brayton who lived on Harrison, a short distance away from her.

"I have everything I need for a great story, but now my question is, should I write it? Obviously the railroad went to great pains to keep Mr. Lincoln's visit from the general public or mostly from enemies of the railroad. Lincoln's whole reason from coming was to get firsthand information for his upcoming case. The official title is Hurd versus the Rock Island Railroad. Will my publishing it give away Mr. Lincoln's hand? It would certainly be a great scoop. The Republican Party will be especially upset, because he didn't let them know, after he said he might combine a talk with his research. But again, that was last year before the elections. Colleen, I trust your instincts. What do you think?"

Colleen felt the blood rushing to her face. It was such an important decision.

"Tom, much as I know how disappointed you will be not to print the story, it seems for the sake of the bridge outcome, you should forget it. No, on second thought, write it up, but store it away for future generations to read. Or, after the trial is over – did you say it starts on the 22nd of September? – you can publish it. That way you can get a good night's sleep tonight and possibly help Mr. Lincoln win his case on the 22nd, by not letting his opposition know just how well-prepared he is."

That is what Tom did.

Chapter 31
UNDERGROUND RAILROAD
Monday, 14 September 1857

Every day in the newspapers there were articles and often at school there were discussions about slavery. One of Colleen's classmates was from the South and believed in owning slaves. It was a part of his life and he considered slaves as possessions to be owned. Colleen felt that to be wrong. Every human being is made in God's likeness, has a soul and should be free, she reasoned. Her family had felt the repression in Ireland before coming to the United States. She was only eight when they left, but she remembered a little of what it was like.

Slavery was becoming more and more a national issue, even though James Buchanan tried to suppress it. The Kansas-Nebraska Act of 1854 provided that Kansans should vote for or against slavery when adopting a state constitution, and at the moment Kansas had two different state governments, one pro-slavery and one against. Troops were sent in to maintain order. This was the situation that Buchanan inherited in 1857.

"Colleen, I know you are against slavery, but would you be willing to help a Negro person to freedom, if he asked you?" This was the question that Tom proposed to her as they walked along the street outside the library.

"What a strange question!" responded the sixteen-year-old. After some thought, Colleen answered "I suppose I would, but that will never happen. Besides, what could I do?"

Then Tom proceeded to tell her that on this very day there might be a slave hidden in someone's house here in Davenport who was on his or her way to Canada. "There are those who are always on the lookout for runaway slaves, or the money they would get for finding them," said Tom. "So runaways are always kept very secret. It is called the Underground Railroad, people who help slaves get to freedom." This was the first that Colleen had heard of the Underground Railroad.

That evening, Colleen asked her parents if they knew of the existence of this secret means of helping slaves escape from the South. James had heard of it because it had come up in conversations with his friends. Maura and he had discussed it between themselves, but had never thought it something to talk to the children about. At sixteen, Colleen was old enough to know and they were glad she brought it up. "Yes, we are very sympathetic to these slaves, many of whom are mistreated and beaten. The river is one way they are transported. It is a dangerous thing for any slave who is caught or for the person who helps him or her. Harboring a runaway is breaking the law today, because these people are considered property in the South. How did you learn of this?"

"Tom Gannon told me today after researching the presidential candidates in the library. He knows things like this because that is his job to know," said Colleen. "However, the Underground Railroad is not something he can write about in the newspaper, at least not now. It will have to be a long time from now when slavery is abolished. Papa, do you think that will ever happen?" Colleen asked sincerely.

"Yes, the good Lord will see to it, Colleen, I'm sure. The country is so divided over this, though, that I'm afraid it might get worse before it gets better. But it is bedtime for you, my dear," James said as he gave Colleen a kiss on the cheek.

It was several weeks later, when Colleen saw Mrs. Dray, a teacher she knew come out of one of her neighbor's houses. Colleen was surprised to see her and ran to catch up to her. However, Mrs. Dray didn't see Colleen and got into her carriage and started down Harrison Street hill in a hurry with the horses and wheels raising a cloud of dust that almost choked Colleen.

The Kanes had lived in the neighborhood now for two years and knew most of the neighbors. But the people in the house that Mrs. Dray had visited were newcomers to the area. Colleen kept hoping that a girl her age would move in.

It was her chance the very next day as she was walking past the green-colored Victorian style house. It had a tower on the third floor and a large front window with Irish lace curtains which Colleen thought might indicate that they were Irish. A heavy-set woman came out from the house, dressed up with hat and shawl and carrying an umbrella for the sun. She didn't see Colleen coming.

"Good afternoon, ma'am," said Colleen as they met at the point where the brick walk from the green house met the wooden street walk. "I'm Colleen Kane, one of your neighbors. Welcome to the neighborhood!"

The woman was very surprised at the greeting and said, "Glory be to God, my child. How nice of you! My name is Katie O'Toole." With a broad smile that made Colleen glad she had spoken, Katie asked, "And where might you live, Colleen Kane?"

Colleen pointed out her house back up the hill about half a block. "Do you have children?" Colleen asked. "I saw Mrs. Dray leaving your house yesterday, and as she is a teacher, I thought maybe you had children. I was hoping to find a neighborhood girl about my age."

"I'm sorry," said Mrs. O'Toole. "My children are grown up and live out East. My husband is a riverboat pilot and was offered a job here on the Mississippi River so we moved here. Mrs. Dray is an old friend," she explained.

"What a coincidence that your husband should be a riverboat pilot. We just met Daniel Smith Harris. Do you know him?" Colleen was now quite excited.

"No, we are just new to the area."

By this time the two had walked down the hill and were in the commercial area on 2nd Street. They each had separate agendas – Colleen was going to the newspaper office to see Tom and Mrs. O'Toole to the Book and Stationery Store. They exchanged farewells with the intent of seeing one another soon.

Tom was glad to see Colleen and very interested when she told him all the recent news of meeting Captain Harris and now Mrs. O'Toole. "I was so hoping that she might have a girl my age, especially when I saw Mrs. Dray leaving her house yesterday."

Tom's ears perked up. "Mrs. Dray, the teacher, was at her house?" he asked incredulously.

"Yes, she said they were old friends."

"But, Colleen, the Drays are from this area all their lives, and you said the O'Tooles are from the East. I wonder when they got to be 'old friends?'" murmured Tom, almost under his breath.

"And, Tom, you won't believe this, but Mr. O'Toole is a riverboat pilot, but being new, they don't know Captain Harris."

"That is very understandable. Captain Harris is well-known in the Midwest – on the Ohio, the Missouri, as well as on the Mississippi River and its smaller tributaries – but is not likely known in New York and places east."

"When I tell Mamma about our new neighbor, I'm sure she will want to have her over for tea, especially since she is from Ireland, too. They will have so much in common."

Tom was about to go out on an assignment. They left the office together, and in parting Tom said, "Colleen, find out all you can about the O'Tooles, but don't let anyone know you are curious. Something about them is mysterious. Maybe it is just my being a reporter, but I think there is a story here."

When they parted, Colleen felt excited. She couldn't wait to tell her mother about the O'Tooles and to find out more about her mysterious neighbors.

Chapter 32
KATIE O'TOOLE
Sunday, 20 September 1857

Colleen was correct in thinking her mother would invite Katie O'Toole for tea. Maura was excited to find fellow countrymen living so close. She wondered what county in Ireland they were from and when they had arrived in the States. "First thing next week, you can deliver an invitation to tea," said Maura, smiling at her daughter.

At Sunday Mass at St. Margaret's Church on the hill, Maura gave thanks to God for all the blessings that she had been given – the children, their health, their being free in the United States away from the poverty and deprivation of her homeland, and for the steady work that James now had at the newspaper.

Maura was deep in her prayer of Thanksgiving when Antoine LeClaire and his wife, Marguerite, arrived. James, on the end of the aisle, nodded and spoke quietly to the LeClaires. Antoine responded also in hushed tones, "It is so nice seeing you and your family, James. What are you doing these days? I haven't seen you in a while."

But just then the priest came out onto the altar to begin Mass and the LeClaires found their seats and all stood for the celebration. There was no time to answer. Colleen and Erin had been on the inside of the pew, poking each other, until Maura stopped them with a hard look.

At the sermon, Colleen looked around a little. Three pews to the front was a heavyset woman that she recognized. It was Mrs. O'Toole with a man Colleen assumed was her husband. Colleen wanted to point them out to her mother but this was not the time. Colleen wanted desperately to tell her mother, but she waited until Mass was over and people were leaving.

"Mamma, Mamma, there is Mrs. O'Toole, our neighbor." Colleen tried to point her out with the crowds exiting, but she saw her only for a moment, then she vanished. "I don't know what happened to her," Colleen said, very surprised. She had to console herself that her mother would have to wait to see Mrs. O'Toole when she came to tea.

It was Wednesday that Mrs. O'Toole agreed to visit the Kanes. She had seemed quite hesitant when Colleen delivered the invitation. Mrs. O'Toole invited Colleen into her sunny front parlor where she read Maura's note. "Heavenly days, Child, your mother has invited me for tea. How nice of her!" Colleen could tell that Mrs. O'Toole was thinking hard by the way she was blinking her eyes fast and frequently. It was a trait Colleen had noticed in others, but it was very obvious in this new neighbor. Mrs. O'Toole finally agreed to Wednesday at 2 p.m., since Maura had left the date and time up to her.

Wednesday turned out to be a beautiful summer day with a slight breeze. Mrs. O'Toole arrived punctually at 2. Colleen answered the front door with her mother and introduced the two ladies to each other. "Mrs. O'Toole, this is my mother, Maura Kane. Mamma, this is our new neighbor, Mrs. O'Toole."

Extending her hand, Maura said, "Welcome to our house and neighborhood, Mrs. O'Toole. May the blessings of God be with you and yours."

"Thank you very much. The same to you." As she came in, Mrs. O'Toole said, "Glory be to God, but you have done a good job with this child, Maura. May I call you that? Please call me Katie." The two ladies got along very well right from the start.

"Colleen told me that you have two grown children out East. Is that correct?"

"Yes, Patrick is 22 and Brigit is 20. They are together in our house in a small town in New York. They didn't want to come West with us when my husband accepted the job here that Fred Dray told us about," Mrs. O'Toole answered. "Do you know the Drays?"

"Yes, my husband worked for the railroad and has known Fred Dray. His wife is Colleen's teacher in high school. Colleen said that she saw Mrs. Dray leaving your house just last week. Are you close friends?"

Colleen was especially interested in Mrs. O'Toole's answer. By this time, Colleen's mother had the fresh tea made and poured for the three of them. She had earlier made scones to serve with it, and Colleen now passed the tray of them to Mrs. O'Toole and her mother.

To Colleen it seemed that Mrs. O'Toole was a little uncomfortable as she answered. "Yes, and she had come to welcome us when Colleen saw her. Maura, your scones are delicious. There is nothing like a good Irish scone, I always say."

"Colleen, my dear, what do you want to be when you grow up?" Mrs. O'Toole had changed the subject.

Colleen said, "I plan to be a writer, ma'am."

Then it was Colleen's turn to ask Mrs. O'Toole a question. "Last Sunday, I saw you at St. Margaret's but when I wanted to speak to you, I couldn't find you. You just seemed to disappear."

Again Mrs. O'Toole seemed uncomfortable. "My husband and I were in a hurry and we left by the side door," she responded.

"We didn't think we knew anybody well enough to stop and talk. I didn't see you there."

Just then Erin came into the room. Mrs. O'Toole said, "Oh, I see you have a brother, Colleen." Maura introduced Erin and the conversation turned to him and the weather.

"I'll be off now," said Mrs. O'Toole. "I have many things to do in getting settled and my Mike will be home this evening. He is a riverboat pilot and is often gone for days on the river, but not tonight. Thank you so much for the tea, Maura. Faith and begorrah, but it is nice to have such thoughtful neighbors. I'll have to have you to my house when I am all settled. Thank you again." Mrs. O'Toole was already at the door and was leaving.

Maura said, "I had hoped we'd get to know one another better, but if you must leave . . ." Her words were hardly heard by the woman as she hurried down the walk.

Colleen couldn't wait to tell Tom that there was something truly mysterious about this woman. She seemed to be hiding something, but what?

Chapter 33
COFFINS
Monday, 21 September 1857

Tom was on assignment. He was covering a talk being given in St. Anthony's Church, a general meeting place until a more public place could be built. The guest speaker was from the University of Iowa. The University, which was founded in 1847 but did not offer its first classes until 1855, was issuing its first degree this spring – a Bachelor of Science degree. The University was opening its Museum of Natural History in Iowa City. The speaker was here to promote the institution of higher learning and to answer questions from prospective students. Not only was this newsworthy, but it also was of interest to Tom personally. He would inquire about degrees they offered in writing or journalism. Although he wasn't eager to leave his job, Davenport and his friends, he knew that he had much to learn if he were to be a publisher of a newspaper someday.

He was too early for the meeting, so he went down to the river to cool off from the summer heat. There was always a breeze on the riverfront. He watched the small boats with fishermen in them. They seemed to be catching nothing but someone on the riverbank had a bite. He watched as an elderly man pulled in a large fish with a snout shaped somewhat like a paddle. Not being a fisherman himself, he was curious as to what it was called. He asked the gentleman, who said it was a "paddlefish." Tom wasn't sure if that was a name he just gave it or was really a type of fish.

Next his attention was drawn to the large packet boat, the *Dr. Franklin*, that traveled from St. Louis to St. Paul regularly carrying passengers, cargo and mail. It was one of the many boats seen docking weekly at the levee in Davenport or Rock Island. Tom knew that Antoine LeClaire had, no doubt, been there to meet the *Franklin* when it arrived that afternoon. All was quiet now because the passengers had disembarked and the commodities that arrived on the boat had been unloaded on the levee awaiting pickup. What Tom thought was unusual was the captain talking to Fred Dray on the brick levee. The two men appeared to be having a serious conversation before the riverboat captain returned to his boat and Dray left on a large horse-drawn flatbed wagon going west, not toward the bridge and his home, as one might expect. It puzzled Tom for a moment, but it was about time for the University meeting. So he turned and hurried the few blocks to St. Anthony's.

The meeting was pretty crowded with mostly men, young and middle-aged. There were a few women who attended all events to claim women's rights, and to his surprise, Colleen was among them. With his 'press' card in his cap and small notepad and pencil in hand, he went up to her and said teasingly, "Miss, may I interview you for the *Davenport Gazette*?"

She jumped from surprise when Tom greeted her because she had not been expecting to see him. She went right along with the farce, "I think I might be able to do that. What would you like to ask?"

His face was aglow with pleasure both at seeing her and at her going along with his joke. Then they both laughed and hugged for the first time. It was an automatic response to the moment, but one that made both think again of how they each viewed the other. Therefore, as they separated, Tom thought, "Colleen, you really do make me feel good, I would really miss you if I went off to school for four years."

Colleen felt somewhat embarrassed and shy to have hugged a man in public and yet it made her feel wonderful. She always felt so warm and happy when she was around Tom. Her heart was pounding.

The meeting started just then and everyone sat down, Tom and Colleen near the front. The speaker – Amos Dean, president of the university – told about the advantages of the big university and of the courses and degrees being offered. Tom was able to ask his question about journalism and English degrees but was disappointed by the speaker's face as he responded. "We have a department of Modern Languages, which would include English, of course, but no courses in journalism per se," said Mr. Dean with a note of disdain. "However, as time goes on we will be adding other courses and degrees." Colleen had the same question, but was surprised that Tom was thinking of going to the University of Iowa. "Wouldn't it be nice if we both could go," she thought, but she had two more years of high school and had no money to pay for college.

After the gathering ended, it was dark outside and Colleen was happy to have Tom to escort her home. He suggested that they walk to the levee to enjoy the cool breeze. She was thinking shyly of romance, but he had something else in mind. He told her then of what he had seen before. As they crossed the gaslighted Second Street, a number of couples in carriages with lanterns passed. It was a lovely summer night. Tom and Colleen headed for Front Street where they saw the *Dr. Franklin* still anchored. On the sloping cobblestone levee stood a lone horse and wagon, the same one that Tom had seen before, now loaded with bundles of straw. The driver was not with it. There were, however, many people walking on the levee – couples both old and young, dog owners as well as men alone, one of which was Fred Dray. He was standing by a railing a little ways beyond the large boat, just watching the river flow.

"Something is going to happen," Tom asserted. "But what?" He was sure that it would be when all these people were gone. So he walked Colleen home and then came back to the office to write up his story. "University of Iowa Confers Degree" was his caption. It was hard for him to concentrate on the story. "Thursday evening, before a packed house, officials announced the first degree for the University of Iowa, in Iowa City, former capital of the state, will be conferred this spring."

The editor came in at that point, having seen the light in the office at this late hour. It was 10:30 p.m. and not unusual, but he wondered which of his reporters was working overtime.

"Tom!" he exclaimed, "I didn't think your assignment was that important that you would need to write it up tonight."

"Mr. Sanders, I knew that I wouldn't be able to sleep, so I decided to do it now." Tom couldn't tell of the suspicious goings-on at the riverfront. He had no proof or clue as to what it was. How could he tell anyone? "I just got here, so I may be here a while," Tom elaborated, thinking midnight or after would be when events would happen at the river.

"That is fine, just don't forget to put out the lamp when you leave." Mr. Sanders left the office and the building.

It was midnight when Tom turned in his story on the editor's desk and left the office to go to the riverfront again. Fred Dray's wagon was still there, loaded with bales of straw and a dark oilskin cover in case of rain. Everything was quiet, so Tom entertained himself by skipping stones out across the water. He had become proficient at this when he was younger. It didn't take long for the skill to return. Of course, the small stones did not travel very far over the wide Mississippi before giving way to gravity.

A slight breeze was creating waves that lapped against the shore with a rhythmic sound. Tom was standing in the shadow of a tree and hid himself behind the tree trunk when he heard a noise coming from the *Franklin*. The gangplank had been left down, possibly for the convenience of passengers who stayed out late. One such person was returning while singing boisterously "Oh My Darling Clementine" and staggering up the plank. At one point Tom saw him teeter and almost fall. But he regained his balance and continued onto the boat. A ship's hand, on watch, assisted him and tried to keep him quiet so others could sleep.

Then things were quiet again.

About an hour later, Tom was sitting on the ground, almost falling asleep under the starry but moon-free sky, when he saw some movement by the top of the gangplank. Two men in dark clothing came down the plank carrying what appeared to be a coffin. It was a simple raw wood box but must have been heavy the way they handled it. They headed directly for the wagon with the straw. One man put his coffin-end down and pulled a heavy narrow plank from the wagon and they slid the box up onto the flatbed between bales of hay. Then they went back onto the boat and repeated the process three more times with more coffins. "It looks as though there were a lot of deaths in someone's family, or are those boxes holding something else?" Tom wondered.

After all were loaded, one man went back onto the *Franklin* while the other unhitched the horse, climbed into the driver's seat and headed north. "It had to be Fred Dray," Tom said to himself. Now Tom had no horse of his own to ride and thought better of borrowing one from the *Gazette* at this hour. His only alternative was to follow in the shadows of the gas-lighted streets on foot. However, when the downtown buildings ended, his cover was gone. The wagon turned up Harrison Street which was dry but rutted. He was not surprised to see the vehicle turn again near the Kane home more than halfway up the hill. But Tom was city blocks behind the wagon and lost sight of it completely. He ran on the brick walk in the open now, knowing he would not be seen by the driver. Tom was sure he knew where Fred Dray was headed with the coffins but he had to see with his own eyes.

For the second time that night Tom arrived at the Kane household. But it was all dark this time and from behind a large bridal wreath bush in the front yard he could look down the hill to the back of the O'Tooles' house. Standing there, silhouetted against a white barn, was the horse-drawn wagon piled with straw bales. Within minutes someone from inside the house came out and together the two men slide one box down the board ramp and carried it inside the house. Then they returned for a second. Tom couldn't see every movement in the dark but he knew the procedure.

It took a very short time for this unloading and the Dray wagon was again on its way. However, this time Fred Dray went down the hill in his horse-drawn vehicle with two coffins still aboard.

Tom had seen enough. He headed for home.

Chapter 34
A STATION
Wednesday, 23 September 1857

Colleen hadn't seen Tom for a few days. She was working on a sampler that she had started when they first moved into their house on Harrison. She had drawn their new house and a picture of each of the family members holding hands. It was fun using different stitches she had learned at school – outline stitch, French knots, cross-stitch, feather stitch – in many colors. She wore a pink dress on the sampler, Erin was in yellow and grey, Mama had on a beautiful long full blue dress and Papa was stitched in a green shirt and brown vest and pantaloons. She was thinking of her hope chest these days and wanted to finish this before starting on towels and pillow slips which she had been given as gifts.

It was the librarian, Mr. Hundgate, who told Colleen when she made her daily visit, that Tom had been looking for her. But before she could gather her things to go find him, Tom arrived. He indicated for her to come between the book stacks and he whispered, "Colleen, I have lots to tell you. I think your neighbors, the O'Tooles, are running a 'station' on the Underground Railroad and Fred Dray is a 'conductor'."

These terms meant nothing to Colleen, so he explained. "People are helping the slaves in the South to escape to Canada by rail, boat, buggy or whatever. They are moved from a house in one town to a house in another. The route is called "the Underground Railroad."

"Yes, you told me all of that," said Colleen impatiently.

"Anyone who helps a runaway slave on this route is called a 'railroad worker.' Someone who leads them from place to place is a 'conductor.' Finally, someone who feeds and gives shelter is a 'station master' and the place is a 'station,'" explained Tom.

Colleen was amazed at this information. She asked, "But how do you know all of this about the O'Tooles and Mr. Dray?"

Tom explained that he had waited last Saturday by the steamboat, and told her about seeing the four coffins.

Colleen broke in here to say that she was sorry that someone had died. She wondered who it might be and why would he be so secretive about it.

Tom didn't comment, but continued, "The two men went back on the

boat and hid the coffins among the straw, covering all with oilskin. Then
Fred Dray drove the horse and wagon up Harrison Street to the
O'Tooles'.

Colleen's eyes were wide open. "Tom," she almost screamed, but
realized that they were still in the library.

"They unloaded two coffins at the O'Tooles' house and Dray left with
the other two. But that isn't all. Yesterday in the *Gazette* was an ad, the
likes of which I have seen before. I cut this one out for you to see."

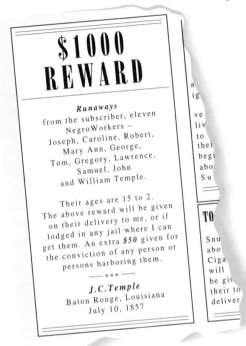

> # $1000
> # REWARD
>
> *Runaways*
> from the subscriber, eleven
> NegroWorkers –
> Joseph, Caroline, Robert,
> Mary Ann, George,
> Tom, Gregory, Lawrence,
> Samuel, John
> and William Temple.
>
> Their ages are 15 to 2.
> The above reward will be given
> on their delivery to me, or if
> lodged in any jail where I can
> get them. An extra *$50* given for
> the conviction of any person or
> persons harboring them.
> — *** —
>
> *J.C.Temple*
> Baton Rouge, Louisiana
> July 10, 1857

Colleen read the article and was amazed. "Do you really think they
are in the coffins?" she asked wide-eyed. "How sad!"

"I am almost sure," answered Tom. "But no one else must know
because of the Fugitive Slave Law. That law says that Northerners must
return runaway slaves or face imprisonment or pay a fine of $1,000.
Some people even seek out runaways to get the reward."

"How awful!" whispered Colleen.

The librarian was picking up books and returning them to the shelves
getting ready to close. The two young people left in deep thought.

"For the moment you must not tell anyone, not even your parents,
Colleen," warned Tom as they walked down the noisy street.

That was going to be hard because she was in the habit of discussing everything with her folks to help make her decisions. However, she knew he was right. Tom had no proof it was the runaways in the caskets, and secondly, it is a serious offense, and the wrong person must not hear about it, if true.

"What are we going to do?" asked Colleen.

"Wait and watch!" was Tom's answer. "You are in a perfect position to see what is going on in the O'Tooles' backyard. If something looks suspicious, let me know."

"But Tom, how can I let you know at midnight or later?" questioned Colleen with a frown and wide eyes. "We don't have one of those new-fangled telephones. Even if we did, they say the operator often listens in."

Tom had no answer to that question. She would have to play it by ear, but hopefully that would not happen.

A very ordinary summer day for Colleen went as follows. She usually awakened by 8 a.m., dressed, and ate her breakfast. She loved oatmeal and milk in the morning. Then it was chore time. She was responsible for dusting the furniture and the floors because horses and carriages of any kind driving by raised dust that came in through "the cracks," it seemed. That was a problem that the city was working on and was starting to fix by paving the streets with brick. Cleaning the outhouse was her other task. She thoroughly washed the floor and two-hole seats once a week, usually on Monday. She used the hot water that Mamma had at the end of washing the family clothes to disinfect "one of the most important rooms in the household," as Papa called it. It was also her duty to see that a catalog or corn husks were plentiful.

If she had time then she walked to the library. Mr. Hundgate still let Colleen take books home with the understanding that they be returned in a week, unless someone asked for them before that. After lunch, her time was free to write in her journal, read or work on her embroidery. Her sampler was now finished so she was starting a pillow slip with a border of flowers. She often went back to the library or stopped at the newspaper office to see Tom in the afternoon.

The day Tom told her the news about the eleven runaway slaves, Colleen walked home thinking how difficult it must have been for all the children to survive in those coffins even for a short time, especially the littlest ones. Nothing looked out of the ordinary at the O'Tooles' as she passed by. No one was peeking out from around the curtains nor was there any unusual sound. She really wanted to go up to the door and say, "Mrs. O'Toole, please let me help with those children. I know your secret. We have toys that they can play with and, I am sure, some food to help feed them." However, Colleen knew that was not what she should do, so she continued home.

That night she dreamed that she was on a train down South and as it was stopped, she saw a slave owner with a number of black children, whose hands were tied behind their backs, getting off the train. One of the bigger boys started to run toward a group of trees and the white man started after him with a whip. Just as he was raising the instrument to strike the teen, Colleen woke up screaming, "No!" She was in a cold sweat as she sat up in bed. The dream had been so real.

The sound of her outcry brought her mother to her room. "It is all right, Colleen," Maura was saying as she brushed Colleen's sweaty black hair from her wet forehead and put her arm around her. "It's all right," she repeated. "It was just a bad dream. Try to go back to sleep."

"But, Mamma, I don't think I can!" replied Colleen.

Sensing something more was bothering her daughter, Maura said, "Do you want to tell me about it?"

Then Colleen told her mother the whole story of the strange actions of Mr. Dray, the bridge operator, down by the river; of Tom watching men taking four coffin-shaped boxes off the packet boat and loading them on Fred Dray's wagon and finally Mr. Dray delivering two of them to the O'Tooles' house at two in the morning.

"Praise be to God, Colleen, there must have been some big catastrophe to have four coffins. But why the secrecy and what happened to the other two coffins?" asked Maura.

"We don't know about the other two boxes, but a few days later Tom cut out an ad from the newspaper. It offered a reward for the return of eleven runaway slave children ages 2 to 15. We know it is all circumstantial, but it fits together so perfectly, Mamma. Can you imagine all those little ones cramped up together in coffins?"

"Now wait a minute, Colleen, you do not know that this is the case. Suppose they are real coffins for relatives who died of a contagious disease or big fire or something? What you need to do is get the facts straight. Maybe I can find out more. I owe Katie a visit anyway. Now you get some sleep and we'll talk more about it tomorrow." Maura got Colleen to lie down and she tucked her in like she used to do. It wasn't long before Colleen was sound asleep.

But now it was Maura who couldn't sleep. She was mulling over all that she had just heard. Could she really find out anything from Katie? How could she broach the subject? She told herself that she would think of something tomorrow and finally dozed off to sleep.

The next morning, after James went to work, Maura had no further clue as to what she would say to Katie O'Toole. She wanted to talk to James about it, but decided she would wait until after she visited her neighbor. It was Wednesday and the day she regularly ironed. However, she could think better seated, so she would mend instead. There was always that basket of socks to be repaired and a jacket of Erin's that was torn.

She had gotten Erin up; Colleen woke up on her own. They had their breakfast together. Maura had another cup of tea while the children ate their porridge. Maura heated water for the dishes, and sent Erin to get dressed and then out to weed the vegetable garden. "He knows now which are plants and which are weeds, thank goodness," she thought.

Colleen was anxious to talk when Erin was outside. "What are you going to say to Mrs. O'Toole, Mamma?"

"I don't know, Colleen, but I'll bring the conversation around to something involving the runaway slaves or slavery in general. There is the Dred Scott Decision of last year – you know that Scott lived in Davenport for a while – the Fugitive Slave Act of 1850 which changed a lot of people's opinion, or even the book, *Uncle Tom's Cabin*." Maura had a great empathy for the black people because she, like all the Irish, had felt the oppression of the English, but that was something she did not like to talk about. "I don't think I will have any trouble."

Shortly after lunch, Maura washed up and put on a flowery summer dress that she had made for herself. It had a little standup lace collar on a fitted bodice coming to a point in front below the waist, with a lightly gathered skirt of the same material. The white background and bright flowers set off her shiny black hair, which she drew up into a bun. A simple small light green hat that matched the green in the dress completed her special outfit.

It took but a few minutes for Maura to walk to the O'Tooles' house. She knocked at the front door and thought she heard a scrambling sound before Katie opened the door. "Glory be to God, if it isn't Maura Kane!" she exclaimed, looking truly surprised. "To what do I owe this pleasant surprise? Come in, come in!" Katie seemed to be speaking unusually loudly, Maura thought.

"I baked these brownies yesterday and thought you and Mike might enjoy some," said Maura as she entered the parlor. The room was quite stark with few pieces of furniture – several ladder-back chairs, an upholstered couch and rocking chair and a side table with flowers probably from her pretty gardens outside. It was sunny and bright with the white Irish-lace curtains at the window and the bare wooden floor.

"It has been a week since you visited me, and we didn't have much time to talk, so I thought I should return the favor. How do you like Davenport by now?" Maura started the conversation as she sat down on the high-backed chair and handed the plate of goodies to Katie.

"How sweet of you to bring us brownies, Maura. Thank you." Katie put the treat on the table next to the flowers and sat down. "We are settling into the area very well, thank you."

"Do you think very often of your life in Ireland?" she began. "I know whenever I hear about the slaves in the South, I feel for them. Our life in Ireland was oppressed by the English and though we didn't live with whips, we knew they were always present waiting, wanting and ready to collect." Maura was starting to tear up even after eight years of freedom in America.

"Blessed be God, but it is good to hear someone expressing the same way I feel. Yes, we felt as though the thumb of the English was on us all the time. For that reason, plus we feel no man can own another body and soul, my husband and I are certainly against slavery here in this country. Does that mean, Maura, that you are an abolitionist, too?

"James and I have never been active in the movement but certainly are in agreement, especially after the 1850 Fugitive Slave Law was put into effect. When the government tells us that we have to turn in any runaway 'slave' – I don't even like to call them that because they are people – to an owner who beats, sells and often kills them, I object strongly. Have you read that book, *Uncle Tom's Cabin*? It certainly shows what it is like for those poor people."

"I haven't read it, but in New York and Philadelphia, from where we just moved, we were involved in the 'Underground Railroad.' Do you know what that means, Maura?" Katie knew she was possibly telling more than she should, but she felt confident that her neighbor might join them.

"Really?" exclaimed Maura almost in a whisper. "You mean you have actually helped some of these people escape bondage?" She was truly impressed because that meant that the O'Tooles had had experience in helping runaways. Now all she needed was to get Katie to admit that she has some slaves hiding in her house at this moment.

Suddenly there was a noise and a muffled cry from upstairs.

Katie knew that Maura had heard the cry and felt that she must tell all. "We actually moved here to continue to help others escape, Maura. I am sure, because of what you have said, you will be truly careful about telling anyone else." Katie continued, "Almost as soon as we arrived in Davenport, we heard of a black woman who had eleven children whom she sent on the 'railroad' to escape a cruel owner. We have five of them here now."

"Glory be to God! Can that be true? You have five children in this house at this moment? I can hardly believe that!" Maura feigned disbelief.

"In order not to be discovered, they hid in coffin boxes coming off the steamboat. Even though they were cramped up like that for only a few hours, two or three children in one, they are not looking forward to doing it again. One of the children took deathly sick after arriving here so we have had them for four days. Otherwise they would have moved on the next night." Katie felt very relieved to tell someone whom she knew she could trust.

"Those poor children!" exclaimed Maura. "How could they breathe stuffed in like that, Katie?"

"Through holes that were driven in the coffin sides near their faces. These openings were partially covered with torn labels on the outside." Katie didn't want to give away any more people involved. Maybe at another time she might mention Fred Dray, but not now.

"Is there anything I can do to help, Katie? Erin and Colleen have toys..." but she was cut off by another sound from upstairs. This time it was a loud thump.

Mrs. O'Toole thought they should check. They went to the hallway and pulled down a drop staircase and hurried up them. What Maura saw was shocking.

The hot, stench-filled attic had been made into a dormitory. Small windows at either end provided enough light to see on the bare wide-board wooden floor, where there were straw pallets creating beds for the five children. Four of these mattresses were lined up in a row, covered with a sheet and blanket. But one was laid alone, opposite the others, with a child still on it. That was Samuel, the 5-year-old, who had been sick since he arrived. Katie had diagnosed it as dysentery, a malady not hard to detect. Although the popular treatment was blood-letting by a doctor, she could not call a doctor in this situation.

Katie did everything she could to keep things sanitary so that the rest of Samuel's family would not become ill. Instead of using the outhouse, because it involved going outside, she had provided a pail for the other children and a separate one, covered and isolated, for Samuel.

These were stored back in the eave area of the attic. A screen gave a little privacy. The child was groaning in terrible pain and Caroline, his 14-year-old sister, was bending over him. The three and four-year-olds were looking on, huddled against Joseph, the oldest. They looked frightened to see their brother in such pain and now to see a stranger come up the drop stairway.

Katie relieved their minds by saying that Maura was a friend and introduced each child to her. Immediately Maura went to Samuel and eased Caroline away so that she could get close to test the child's forehead.

She took charge immediately. "Glory be to God, Katie, this child is burning up. We need cool water and a cloth. Joseph, open the windows. The rest of you children should go downstairs with Caroline. Everything is going to be all right!" But Maura wasn't so sure about that.

Maura had always thought she would like to have been a nurse. This was a situation in which she wished she had more training. She took the sheet and blanket off the child and cooled his head and whole body bathing him with the water and cloth that Katie brought. All of this made Samuel feel more at ease but did not relieve the pain.

Joseph wanted to do anything he could to help. Being the oldest, though only fifteen, he felt responsible. Seeing what Maura was doing gave him assurance that he could trust her. He opened up and said, "Samuel wanted to relieve himself and he got up to go behind the screen, but he was too weak... and fell. That is probably what you heard that brought you up here. I carried him back to the mattress. Please don't let anything happen to him." Joseph was almost in tears.

Maura tried to comfort him. "Heavenly days, child, you are all so brave and I know you have done all that anyone can do for your brother. We need to bring his fever down, though, and try to make him comfortable. Why don't you go down with the rest of the children!"

"No, no, no! I must stay with Sammy. He is my little buddy. Mamma put me in charge of seeing that we all get to Canada and that is what I am going to do." Joseph was about in tears.

"May the Blessed Lord help you, child! You may stay. Hand me the bowl of water and I will sponge his little face again." Maura knew she would do anything to help this family now.

But the sponge baths did not bring Sammy's fever down and his pain only grew worse. Maura prayed aloud with Joseph, "Dear Lord, please help this little child. Heal him if it is your will, but please don't let him suffer more. Amen!" Maura's prayer was answered. Samuel died in his brother Joseph's arms a short while later.

It was very sad for all the children. They had been through a great deal together and now death. Joseph took it the hardest. But he was able to explain it to his siblings in a way that Maura had told him. "Samuel now is out of his pain and is with God in heaven. Someday we will all be up there with him."

It was almost dark when Maura left for home. It had been a long day.

The funeral was the strangest ever. Maura went home and sent Colleen to get the priest at St. Margaret's Church to come prepared for a funeral. She left a message for James when he came home from work to come over to the O'Tooles' with a shovel. "Time and secrecy are of the essence," she wrote. She washed and changed her clothes to something a little less festive. Erin was sent to Sean's house.

Back at the O'Tooles' house she and Katie gathered the children in the parlor. Father Andrew Trevis, pastor at St. Margaret's, arrived and was shown the body still in the attic. He gave Samuel a blessing and carried the body down to a make-shift resting place in the parlor. Maura had put a sheet over two chairs with a straw mattress to add some softness. Gently she bathed Samuel's face and hands, thinking she saw a slight smile on the face which before had showed such agony. "Glory be but he must have seen Jesus at the end!" she commented to the French priest as she covered Samuel's tattered clothes with another sheet.

Here the children said their farewells. John and William were in Joseph and Caroline's arms respectively, not really understanding what was going on, but feeling the sadness.

With the sound of much crying in the background, Father Trevis prayed over Samuel and had the children sing songs they knew. Slowly and softly they sang "Swing Low Sweet Chariot," "Jesus Loves Me," which was Samuel's favorite, Joseph said, and finally "Amazing Grace," which left everyone in tears.

Katie said a few words in eulogy. "Samuel was hurting much of the time, yet he smiled when anyone did anything for him. He was a very brave boy. God has received him up in heaven." Father Trevis gave Samuel a final blessing and the ceremony was over. The two women were busy – Katie put together a meal most of which she had already made, while Maura redressed Samuel in some of Erin's outgrown clothes.

Mike O'Toole and James came in during the funeral but afterwards went to the Kanes' basement and put together a small casket. That is where James learned that it was in a coffin-like box in which the children had arrived.

"He was so cramped up with his sister and younger brother you wouldn't believe it possible. But there was not a sound out of any of them before I opened the top. Then there was a lot of rejoicing but quietly so the neighbors wouldn't hear. Poor Sammy didn't join in much, however, because he was already in pain," Mike continued.

Erin arrived home from the Gannons' and, together with Colleen, heard the sawing and hammering in the basement and came down to see what was going on. They were told the full story, much of which Colleen already knew. They were anxious to do anything they could to help. James suggested they find one toy to give to each of the children from among Erin and Colleen's playthings. That the two did, though it was difficult. Most of their toys were special, with special memories, but Samuel's siblings had no toys. Colleen chose a doll that her grandmother in Ireland had made her, and Erin was willing to part with a wooden fire engine from the days when being a fireman was his goal in life. Finding a second toy was harder for each. Colleen wanted something for Joseph. She thought a book would be appropriate since he was 15, but her own library was small so her choices were few. She decided upon a small book of poems by Ralph Waldo Emerson. It had been a gift for her birthday last year. One of her favorite poems called "The Mountain and the Squirrel" she had memorized.

> *The mountain and the squirrel*
> *Had a quarrel,*
> *And the former called the latter "Little prig";*
> *Bun replied,*
> *"You are doubtless very big;*
> *But all sorts of things and weather*
> *Must be taken in together*
> *To make up a year,*
> *And a sphere.*
> *And I think it no disgrace*
> *To occupy my place.*
> *If I'm not so large as you,*
> *You are not so small as I,*
> *And not half so spry;*
> *I'll not deny you make*
> *A very pretty squirrel track.*
> *Talents differ; all is well and wisely put;*
> *If I cannot carry forests on my back,*
> *Neither can you crack a nut."*

The poem helped Colleen to realize that everyone has a different ability. We need not be jealous of someone else, because probably we can do things they can't. Yes, she decided this would be good for Joseph.

Erin looked over his toys and decided on a small ball that he played with a lot but it would be something the little two-year-old could hold and throw.

The small pine coffin was ready and the children wrapped their gifts in newspaper and put them into it in order to carry them more easily. The men tried to camouflage the box to look like a piece of furniture – a chest of drawers carried upright with lines drawn in charcoal for the drawers – if anyone were watching as they carried it to the O'Tooles' household for a simple but ample funeral meal.

Sad as it was for the four runaways, they enjoyed for a few moments the meal and being among loving and giving new friends. Joseph treasured the book of poems, holding it so close to his chest that it would have been difficult to pry it away. Colleen recited her favorite poem for him from memory. She had no idea that Joseph couldn't read. His owner didn't want his slaves educated for fear they would be less dependent on him and seek freedom. But Joseph was so bright that he could almost recite the poem himself having only heard it once.

Caroline, fourteen, had loved a doll that her mother had made for her, but she didn't have time to get it when they left the Louisiana plantation that night that now seemed long ago. She really treasured Colleen's gift that was handmade in Ireland, a country she had never heard about before. It had beautiful braided black hair, with an Irish lace collar on a blue satin dress. The very sight of the doll brought tears of happiness to Caroline's eyes.

John was three, and a very quiet child with very big brown eyes that sparkled when he unwrapped the wooden fire engine. Erin told him what it was and that the cord hose was used to put out fires. He demonstrated making a "shhhhhoo" sound of water to put out the fire. But it was the moving wheels that caused John's face to light up and he pushed the truck round and round. This gift was perfect.

William, at age two, stayed very close to his older siblings. The things that had happened recently – the hasty departure from their mother, the long ride in the hold of the boat with the stench of the animals, using the cargo for seats and beds, being stuffed into a box with his big brother and finally hiding in the O'Toole attic with his sick brother who had died – it was like a bad dream. He had learned on the plantation that crying was not an option. His mother knew that the owner did not like hearing babies cry, so she did everything to stop it happening – she sang to him, rubbed his small back, got Joseph to make funny faces. From the time he was one week old, William lay in the fields alone as his mother and siblings picked cotton. She was only given time twice a day to feed him. Crying would do no good.

Erin handed William his newsprint-wrapped gift to open as the child sat on Joseph's lap. His small hands held it for a minute while he looked hard at the giver. He didn't know this white boy who smiled while handing him something. Joseph told him it was all right to go ahead and open it. His small hands would have dropped it in the process had Joseph not caught it first. But the brown leather rag-filled ball was revealed. What to do with it? First he put it to his mouth, but Erin showed him that it was not to eat, but he could throw and catch it. It didn't take long and he was down on the floor scrambling after it as it rolled. Everyone was in a happier state, but now it was time to eat.

After a rather quiet feast of deer meat, homemade pasta, green beans, corn bread and apple pie, James Kane and Mike O'Toole took Samuel's little body in the new little coffin to the City Cemetery, on the west side of town. There, under cover of darkness, Mike and James dug a grave and buried him. They put a roughly made cross of wood on top with the name "Samuel" carved into it. Although the siblings and Kanes would like to have been there, they would certainly have called attention to themselves, something they could not afford to do. So instead, Father Trevis led them in prayer in the O'Toole parlor.

Two days later in the *Davenport Gazette* was an article entitled, "Mystery Grave Site." It read as follows, "Discovered by the caretaker at Davenport's City Cemetery last evening was a fresh grave marked only by a crude cross carved with the name 'Samuel'. The usual procedure of informing the city clerk and hiring a gravedigger was not followed. Although foul play cannot be ruled out, the Marshal said no fights or other disturbances were reported at the time. He is investigating, but has no leads so far. The grave appears to be that of a child." It was written by Tom Gannon.

Tom knew nothing of the events on Harrison Street until after he had written the article about Samuel. Colleen had come down with a cold the morning after the funeral and stayed in bed most of the day. So it was Friday, the next day, that she informed Tom about the runaways. "Your suspicions were correct," she told him. "Mamma found out because I had a bad dream, couldn't sleep, then told her. I'm sorry, Tom, but she went to see Mrs. O'Toole the next day and let her know that she was sympathetic to the slaves of the South and especially to the runaways. You were right. There were eleven children from one family escaping. Five were in the coffin boxes that you saw come to the O'Toole's, but one was sick. It was poor Samuel, who was only five years old."

The name "Samuel" made Tom's ears perk up. "Samuel was the name on the 'mystery grave,' Colleen. Was this the same child?" asked the reporter.

"Yes, Tom, little Samuel had dysentery, probably from drinking water from a ditch on the plantation where he was picking cotton. But the disease didn't show up until he arrived at the O'Tooles' house. He died while Mamma and Joseph, the oldest runaway child, were with him. The funeral was at the O'Tooles' house. I got Father Trevis, from St. Margaret's, to come to bless him and officiate. Erin and I gave each of the other four children something to play with or take with them on the rest of their journey. They were so grateful and it made them happy for a short time. Oh, Tom, I hope they make it safely the rest of the way to Canada." Colleen was really concerned because she had overheard some men talking on her way to the newspaper office.

One of them had said, "They had better not cross my path or I'll turn them in. Did you see the ad in the *Gazette* offering a reward for their return? It was in again today. I could certainly use the money."

Although no mention was made of runaways, Colleen was sure that what they were referring to was the family of runaways. She looked around as she spoke very softly. "I didn't think people up here in the north would be so cruel. Joseph said that a slave on his plantation was given 550 lashes for running away. Can you imagine that. Tom?" She was about in tears.

Tom, seeing the tears about to flow, put his arm around her to comfort her. "They'll make it, Colleen, they'll make it!" He sounded more positive than he felt.

Chapter 35
MOVING ON
Thursday, 24 September 1857

After the funeral, Mike and Katie O'Toole concentrated on seeing that the children moved safely on to the next 'station' by train. The day that Colleen was sick was a fairly peaceful one for them. Though it was still sad, the Temple family enjoyed the new toys from the Kanes. Katie realized that Joseph could not read so she read some of the poems to him. Again Joseph was so smart that he could repeat the words almost verbatim. But most of his time he spent playing ball with William, who was enjoying seeing Joseph run after the toy.

Katie gave Caroline some material and needle and thread to make more clothes for her new doll. John was going around putting out pretend fires and enjoyed seeing the truck move when he pushed it. The sounds that accompanied this play were often strange but fun for the others to hear.

Evening arrived and Katie informed the children that they would be moving to the next station. "We will be going by train early tomorrow morning to Chicago. So you need to get a good night's sleep."

Fred Dray had informed the O'Tooles that a 5 a.m. train from Rock Island to Chicago would be leaving the Davenport depot at 4:45 a.m. He would be there to pick them up at 3 a.m. Katie would accompany the two coffins of relatives from the East. Medical papers would be forged, indicating the death of her aunt, from natural causes, while visiting the O'Tooles, and of her uncle, dying within a day of heart failure because of his sudden loss. Grieving Katie planned to go back for the funeral in New York. Her husband, Mike, as a riverboat pilot was away on another trip, and he therefore could not be with her.

She would tell this story to anyone who might need to know or who might ask. Katie was dressed all in black with a veil over her face to hide her sorrow. James Kane came to help the children into the coffins at the last minute and to make sure there were air holes by each of their faces. The little ones were not too happy to do this again because they had already experienced the discomfort of the box. Now they would have to be cramped and quiet for a longer time. William at age 2, and John at age 3, could not be expected to keep still for so long a period, so Katie had gotten a sedative from the local druggist for them.

James nailed the pseudo-coffins closed, feeling very sad to see the children leave and anxious for their safety. However, he knew the need for them to move on. The bounty of $1,000 was too enticing a reason for some to pass up if they had any idea of where the runaways were.

When Fred Dray arrived with his empty wagon, the two men loaded the coffins and James helped Katie onto the driver's seat between Fred and himself. "Katie is certainly a brave person," he thought to himself. Aloud he said, "When will you be back, Katie? Are you going all the way to New York?"

"Yes," she replied. "After I see the caskets safely to Chicago, I'm going on to visit my sister in New York. Mike and I decided that I need a rest after the stress of our move here, the children's arrival, the sickness and death of Samuel and, finally, arranging for moving the rest of the children. Besides, if anyone were to check on me, I would need to be gone five or six days. I might just as well spend them with family."

All of this was true, thought James. Katie had been the one with the daily responsibility of hiding the children, feeding, bathing the little ones and nursing Samuel. He was sure that she felt worse about Samuel's death than anyone outside of his siblings because she knew him best and was entrusted with his care. It was good that she was going to have a rest.

As they approached the railroad depot, a one-story log structure at 5th and Farnam which had been given to the railroad by Antoine LeClaire, the area was dark and quiet. James and Fred transferred the coffins from the farm wagon to the railroad cart, which had three other big boxes of different sizes and a bag of mail.

Then Fred Dray drove the horse to a nearby hitching-post and tied him there. James helped Katie down from the high seat to the ground, got her black bag from the wagon bed and walked her into the depot. The waiting room was not that big but had several long benches and a ticket window. Katie got her ticket and showed the papers for the coffins. The ticket master made out a destination label to go on each coffin and went out to attach a label to each. If he noticed that the caskets were going to Chicago and she was going to New York, he made no comment.

As Katie and the two men sat down to wait the train's arrival, a man with a coarse and bloated face, black-beaked hat, rather dirty looking shirt and pantaloons came into the waiting room. The man looked around the room, his eyes passing over the three seated there, and walked over to the ticket window. He asked when the train would arrive. The agent said that it would be on time at exactly 4:45 a.m.

With that answer, he left. James felt uncomfortable, wondering if this man were a bounty hunter.

Other travelers started arriving about 20 minutes before the scheduled departure. A family was seeing the father off to find work in the big city. Two elderly sisters were traveling to Chicago by train for the first time. A younger man brought in their satchels from the top of their carriage and was trying to ease their fears of riding the train. At the last minute, a black man arrived, bought his ticket and stood outside waiting. He apparently was a free man and carried himself with great confidence.

The bounty-hunter suspect came up to the black man as the train was pulling in to the station and asked if he was escorting the coffins. When his answer was, "No," the man turned to the ticket agent, who was now pulling the freight cart toward the end of the train where the mail-car was. He asked who was with the coffins. Being told, "The lady in black," he looked disappointed and left. Katie breathed a sigh of relief.

Chapter 36
INVOLVEMENT
Thursday, 24 September 1857

Boarding the train, Katie found there were many empty seats and she chose the one next to the back of the long passenger car. The last seat was taken. She put her small satchel in the open shelf overhead and sat down facing the way the train was going. The seats could be flipped so that four people could face each other, though half would be riding backwards.

They were crossing the Mississippi River on its first railroad bridge almost immediately after they jerked to a start. Several minutes later they had arrived in Rock Island at a larger depot. Here the passenger car really started to fill up. Families turned the seats and individuals were busy talking as they settled in and stowed their belongings. The passengers became less noisy as the engineer started up again. After a stop in Moline, hot cinders and smoke flew past the windows as they headed east across the prairie in Illinois toward Chicago. The train passed over creeks and through glades of trees, relaxing Katie, almost putting her to sleep. She needed sleep after the last few weeks and this morning's early rise.

Meanwhile, back in Davenport, James Kane and Fred Dray were getting back up on the wagon seat when they noticed the grubby-looking suspected bounty hunter still lurking around.

James said, "Glory be, Fred, I think we were lucky that the black man came when he did. He took the suspicion away from Katie, if there ever had been any. I don't really want to run into that filthy-looking man again. He looks like trouble." Fred agreed and the men left for their respective homes.

Home again, James had some oat porridge with Maura before he headed for work and they discussed the recent events.

"Thank the Good Lord, James, that you were able to help those wee ones to escape. I have been praying my beads ever since you left this morning. Did you run into any trouble?" asked Maura.

"Maura, I'll have a drop more tea," requested James. "We did have a devilish-looking person checking the freight and the passengers. God forbid, but I think he was a bounty hunter. He asked who was accompanying the coffins. When he saw a black man as a passenger, his suspicions were really aroused. But the ticket agent informed him that Mrs. O'Toole was with the caskets. She was very convincing as a mourner, God bless her, and the man left."

Colleen wasn't sleeping well, and having heard her parents talking downstairs, she got up and came down to see what was going on.

"A blessed mornin' to you, Colleen, darlin'!" greeted her father. "Did you sleep well?"

"Mornin'! No, I kept waking up and when I heard you talking, I wondered what was happening so early." Colleen was delighted to hear the news that the Temple children had gotten away on the train even though she knew it would be uncomfortable in the coffin boxes. She was surprised to hear of her father's involvement, but she wasn't told of the bounty hunter since nothing came of it. Maybe now her nights would not be so restless, she thought. She would be sure to tell Tom.

But when she saw Tom, he had news of his own. "Colleen, let's take a walk." When they were walking along the riverfront, he said, "I wanted you to be the first to know. I got a letter from the University of Iowa today accepting me as a student this fall. I plan to give my notice at work right away. What do you think?"

Colleen was taken aback. It was good news for him, she knew, but it took her a minute to catch her breath and say, "Tom, that is wonderful! I'm happy for you." She was pleased to be able to say that. What she wanted to do was to cry. Just a few months ago, before she became sixteen, that was what she would have done, but with all that has happened, she was growing up and taking control of her emotions. "When will you be leaving? Will you be coming home very often?"

Tom noticed tears in Colleen's eyes but said nothing. However, very tenderly he responded that he had a couple of weeks. "I can take the train back and forth so it will not seem that far away. I'll miss you, Colleen! I've never said it before, but my life has been much richer with you in it and I would like to consider you my girlfriend, if that is all right with you."

Now the tears came. Colleen couldn't control them. She couldn't believe her ears. Tom, her best friend, was actually asking to be her beau. "Oh yes, yes!" She threw her arms around him and they kissed. Neither of them cared that people were watching as they passed by.

From that day forward, life in the Kane household seemed different. They had become involved with helping another generation, another culture, make its way to freedom.

It would probably not be their last involvement. Colleen had become a bright young lady with big goals and lots of potential in an age when women were given no power and few rights. Erin was about to become a teenager in this world of unrest and struggle.

For the moment, life was good.

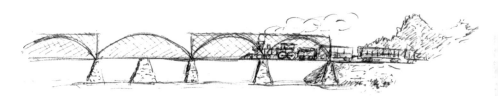

Present and Past Names of Rock Island Streets

Streets		Avenues	
Today	*In the 1850's*	*Today*	*In the 1850's*
1st	Pike, Pine	1st	Mississippi, Water, Front
2nd	St. Clair	2nd	Illinois
3rd	Monroe	3rd	Orleans
4th	Carroll	4th	Rock River
5th	Huron	5th	Moline, Avenue,
6th	Main		Highland, Canal
7th	Pearl	6th	Commercial, Commerce,
8th	Ontario		Pleasant, Green Gable,
9th	Exchange		Grove, Sherman
10th	Ohio	7th	Toledo, Spencer, 7th
11th	Swan	8th	Barnard, Harper,
12th	Otter	8½	Clark
13th	Beaver, Short	9th	Indian Boundary, Prospect
14th	Deer, Stoddard	9½	Toledo, Union
15th	Elk	11th	Atkinson
16th	Buffalo		
18th	Washington		
19th	Jefferson, Cherry		
20th	Madison		
21st	Adams		
22nd	Dock		
23rd	Broadway		
24th	Arsenal		
25th	Davenport, Keokuk		
26th	Stickney, Railroad		
27th	Howard Avenue		
28th	28th		
29th	Columbia, 29th		
30th	Elm		
31st	Andrews		
32nd	Kimbal, 32nd		
38th	Robbins, College Avenue		
42nd	Sylvan, Walnut		
43rd	Francis		
45th	Brooks Avenue		

Glossary

Agenda – a list of things to be dealt with or done

Auger – a tool for boring holes

Beam – a long, thick piece of wood used in building

Cofferdam – a watertight temporary structure in a river for keeping the water from an enclosed area that has been pumped dry

Camaraderie – a sharing of closeness between two or more people; good spirit among comrades

Daguerreotype – a photograph made by an early method on a plate of chemically treated metal or glass

Deck – any platform or floor, like a bridge or ship deck

Drop staircase – wood or metal stairs that fold up into an attic area and can drop down through a doorway in the ceiling

Duress – coercion; the stress that results from being forced to do something unwillingly

Dysentery – a disease of the intestines

Falsework – a temporary scaffolding built of wood or metal to hold a bridge up until it is self-supporting (the intent of falsework is to support the structure, not the workers)

Feign – to pretend or make a false show

Genuflect – to bend the knee, as in worship

Howe Truss – a truss of both wood and metal used by early railroads, designed by William Howe of Massachusetts *(see Truss, below)*

Investigate – search or inquire into

Livery – stable for keeping horses

Mullion – a slender, vertical dividing bar between the panes of glass in a window

Packet boat – a boat that travels a regular route and carries passengers,freight and mail

Pier – a heavy column used to support the weight of a bridge

Pinch bars – a kind of a crowbar with a projection that serves as a fulcrum

Pocket-door – a heavy door that slides between the walls of two rooms

Porridge – a soft food made of oatmeal or other cereal boiled in water or milk

Portico – a porch or covered walk with roof and columns

Root cellar – a space underground used primarily for storing root vegetables

Sampler – a piece of cloth embroidered with designs or letters, to learn various stitches and display skill in needlework

Scaffolding – a temporary framework for supporting men in construction (the intent for scaffolding is to support the workers, not the structure)

Silhouette – a dark shape seen against a light background

Stevedore – a person who loads and unloads ship cargo

Strut – a wood brace fitted into the bridge framework to resist longitudinal compression

Superstructure – that part of the bridge above the deck

Truss – a frame made in the shape of a triangle, the most rigid form of framework

"Costello has written a book that captivates the attention and enjoyment of the tweenager, teenager and the adult reader. The historical background reflects accurately the atmosphere of the time."

> *Dr. Kathleen Eberdt*
> *CHM, Professor Emeritus of History*

"This historical fiction book portrays the hardships and difficulties of life in the 1850's, as well as tells the fun and excitement that were also part of daily living in the Midwest. Readers will gain fascinating historical information leading up to the Grand Excursion of 1854. Those enjoying the Wilder 'Little House' books will like Mississippi River Dreams by Mary Costello."

> *Rochelle Murray*
> *Children's Librarian*

"In her engaging first novel, complete with illustrations, noted Iowa artist and historian Mary Charlotte Aubry Costello has captured both the charm and the challenge of river town life in the tumultuous 1850's as the Kane family, the Midwest and the United States grapple with living up to the promise of freedom for all persons."

> *Suzanne M. Hartung*
> *Educator*